THE GREAT
BLUE YONDER

THE GREAT
BLUE YONDER

by Alex Shearer

AN
APPLE
PAPERBACK

SCHOLASTIC INC.

NEW YORK TORONTO LONDON AUCKLAND SYDNEY
MEXICO CITY NEW DELHI HONG KONG BUENOS AIRES

ISBN 0-439-56127-2

Copyright © 2001 by Alex Shearer. All rights reserved.
Published by Scholastic Inc., 557 Broadway, New York, NY 10012, by arrangement with Houghton Mifflin Company. SCHOLASTIC and associated logos are trademarks and/or registered trademarks of Scholastic Inc.

First published in 2001 in the United Kingdom by Macmillan Children's Books, a division of Macmillan Publishers Limited, 20 New Wharf Road, London, NI 9RR.

12 11 10 9 8 7 6 5 4 3 2 1   4 5 6 7 8 9/0

Printed in the U.S.A.   40

First Scholastic paperback printing, October 2004

to my father

THE GREAT
BLUE YONDER

The Desk

People seem to think it's an easy life when you're dead. But you can take it from me, it's no such thing.

For a start, grownups keep coming up to you and saying, "Oi, you! You're young to be on your own, aren't you? Are you looking for your mum?"

And when you say, "No. She's still alive. I died before she did," they say, "Tut-tut, that's not so good, then," as if there was something you could do about it to change everything, and that it was your fault you weren't still breathing.

In fact, they seem to think that you've even gone and pushed in or something and pinched someone else's place in the queue.

The way people seem to see it here, "over on the other side," as Arthur likes to call it (I'll tell you about Arthur in a minute), is that everything's done according to age and experience—just like at home.

I call it "home," anyway. Arthur calls it "the side." He

says that being alive must be "the side" or else being dead couldn't be "the other side." Well, that's what he says, though it doesn't make much sense to me.

How it seems to work is that you're supposed to have a good long life, and then when you get to be really old, you just sort of fade away and die of nothing in particular. And Arthur says that the best way to do it is to die in bed with your boots on. But I can't quite see what you'd be doing in bed with your boots on—unless you were too ill to take them off. But even then, you'd think that someone would take them off for you. And all I know is that if I'd ever gone to bed with *my* boots on, my mum would have had fifty fits. Sixty fits, maybe. Probably even a hundred fits.

But that's only how it's *supposed* to work. In practice, it doesn't really work like that at all. Because the truth is that people can die at all sorts of ages—young, like me, old, like grandads, or in between, like lots of other people. But if you turn up at the Desk (I'll tell you about the Desk in a minute) and you look like you've gone and died before you were really supposed to, there's all hell to pay. (Not that there really is a hell. Or if there is, I haven't found it yet. As far as I can see, being dead is mostly paperwork.)

So first you die, and then you find yourself in this long queue, and you have to wait your turn to register. And there's a man behind this big desk and he peers down at you through this thick pair of glasses.

"What do *you* want?" he says. "What's a young lad like *you* doing here? *You* can't possibly have had a full life yet. What's your game, then? You've got no business coming here. You should be out on your bike or something."

And then you say, "I *was* on my bike," or however it happened. And he peers at you through his thick spectacles again and says, "You should watch where you're going, then, and be more careful."

And even when you tell him that you *were* watching where you were going and you *were* being careful and it wasn't your fault at all, you still don't get any sympathy.

"You weren't due up here," he says, "for another seventy-two years! You'll play havoc with the computer, you will, getting here before your time. And I've only just got the hang of it. It was all pen and ink and ledgers before, and that was bad enough. I've half a mind to send you back."

But when you say, "OK, fine by me, I wouldn't mind going back, if you can get that truck off me," because you've probably got a lot of unfinished things to do back at home, like homework and stuff, he just looks sad and says, "I'm sorry, son, I can't do it. I only wish I could, but I can't. There's no going back, you see, not once it's happened. Once it's done, it's done, and that's it. You only get the one go. Sorry."

So he fills in the forms and types your name into the computer. And then he gives you a little information sheet about the place—not that it really tells you much. It just says, *Other Lands—Way In*. It doesn't mention a way out. Then there's an arrow with a bubble attached which says, *You are here*. Then there's another arrow with another bubble which says, *To the Great Blue Yonder*. And that's about it.

The Other Lands are a curious place. They're a bit like the saying that something's "neither here nor there." And that's just where they seem to be. They're not exactly here and they're not exactly there, either. But you know they're definitely somewhere, only you couldn't quite put your finger on it or find them on a map. It's a hard thing to describe, really, a bit like trying to explain to someone what it feels like when your leg's gone to sleep. Words don't do it justice somehow. You need to experience it for yourself to know what it really means.

There're lots of trees, though, and paths and long lanes and corners and faraway fields. And every now and then there's a signpost like a big finger, saying, *This way to the Great Blue Yonder* and there're always people heading off in that direction, toward the distant sunset.

But although the sun is always setting, it never quite does disappear. It just hangs there, almost as if time is suspended, like a canopy in the sky. So it's always a glorious color there, all yellows and reds and golds and long shadows. It's like summer and autumn all rolled into one, with a dash of spring for good measure, and hardly any winter at all.

So that's it. There's no real introduction or anything, not like when you first go to school. You just get your information leaflet with the arrow on it pointing to the Great Blue Yonder, and you're more or less on your own. But you don't get lonely because everyone's really friendly and nice to you. Arthur says that this is because we're all in the same boat—dead. (Which is the opposite of a lifeboat, I suppose.)

You get the impression, as you walk about the Other Lands, that most people don't really know what they're doing being dead—just the same as a lot of people in the world didn't know what they were doing being alive. And they go around saying, "What's the meaning of it all? What's the *meaning* of being dead?" Just the same way they used to go around saying, "What's the meaning of life?" and writing books on it. Though it's too late to write books on it now.

When I used to ask my dad questions like this, back when I was alive, he'd just shrug and say, "Don't worry about it, matey, we'll find out when we're dead."

But he was wrong. Because you *don't* find out when you're dead. Because here I am, as dead as half a dozen dodos, totally extinct, and I still haven't got a clue why I'm here or what's really going on. So take it from me, if you're expecting to find out what the meaning of life is once you're dead, you're in for a big disappointment.

Nobody here seems to have a clue what's going on— same as at home. Some people reckon that they'll get to be alive again after a while. I don't know if they will or not. Personally, I have my doubts. And they've forgotten so much about what it was like that they say, "We'll understand what it's all about when we're alive again."

But I don't think they will.

That's one thing about it all—I think that when you've been dead for a long time, your memory starts to go. I think that must be true because I saw old Mrs. Gramley the other morning—who used to live across the street from us—and I went up to say hello to her and to ask her how she was getting on. But she didn't even remember me.

"It's Harry," I said, "from across the street. Don't you remember? You used to take me out in my pram sometimes when I was a baby. And when I started crying, you'd say it was wind, even when it wasn't. Then when I got older, you'd give me chocolate for being good and I wasn't to tell anyone about it. Harry, remember? With the sister. My dad worked for Telecom and my mum worked part-time at the council."

But she just looked at me for a while and said, "I'm sorry, love. I have a vague sort of recollection, but I don't think I know you. Not for sure."

And she went off with her arms stretched out behind her, as if pulling her shopping cart along, just as she always did. Only there was no cart there, except in her imagination. I suppose it was a sort of phantom cart for her really, a ghostly memory of a cart, all full of imaginary bargains and two-for-ones.

When she'd gone, I remembered that she'd died over five years ago. Well, someone can change a lot in five years, and I probably looked nothing like I did the last time we'd met.

But all the same, I was a bit disappointed that she hadn't remembered me. It's not nice when people forget you. You feel like you're disappearing.

I found a few people who remembered me, though: Mr. Barnes, Mr. and Mrs. Gooter, Lesley Brigg, and Auntie Mabe.

Auntie Mabe was very surprised to see me.

"What are *you* doing here, Harry?" she said. "Where's your mum and dad? Shouldn't they have got here first? And why haven't you grown up properly?"

"I was in a bit of trouble," I said. "I had a spot of bother. This accident on my bike. Me and a truck."

"Oh, good gracious!" she said. "I hope it didn't hurt."

And funnily enough, you know, it hadn't. Not a bit. I'd been going along, trying to be careful, not racing or being stupid or mucking about or anything like that, when suddenly this truck appeared from nowhere.

And the next thing I knew—I was here. But it didn't hurt at all. I didn't know a thing. It was like clicking your fingers or turning off the light. One second you're there, next second you've gone. On and off, just like that.

Odd, really. Very odd. Something of a disappearing trick.

I'll tell you something, though—as you're probably wondering—and that's what happens to the babies here. Because, I mean, here I am, and if you could see me, you'd think to yourself, "Well, now, how old is he? Somewhere between ten and twelve, I'd say. Maybe a bit more, maybe a bit less. He could either be a very tall nine or a very short thirteen. But it's plain that he can get around on his own. But what about babies? How do they manage?"

Well, the fact is there's always someone here willing to lend a helping hand if you can't quite cope on your own. Nobody's just abandoned. There's always someone who'll give you a carry and take you along to where you have to go.

It's all very difficult to describe, really. You'd have to be dead yourself to fully understand it. And that would be a bit drastic. I wouldn't go to those lengths. Not if I were you. I mean, there's no hurry to get here, is there? It's not as if you're missing something.

So, anyway. There I am, dead. One moment I've got my whole life ahead of me, next minute I've got my whole death ahead of me. And how long was that going to go on? I mean, what was I supposed to do to fill the time? A bit of painting? Or try and get up a game of football? Or what?

So I go back to the Desk and I ask the man behind the computer terminal there. "Excuse me," I say. "Will I be dead long?"

"Why do you ask?" he says. "Do you have an urgent appointment? Have you got somewhere else to go?"

"Well," I explain, "we had booked a trip to Legoland."

"Tough luck," he tells me.

"Are you dead as well, then?" I ask him. "Are you the Grim Reaper? Is that you, then—Mr. Grim?"

He looks up at me and grunts.

"I'm dead, all right," he says. "Dead tired of answering stupid questions. Now, buzz off and don't annoy me. I'm busy here."

He was, too, as there was a long queue of people waiting to sign in. I saw a few dogs and cats among them as well. I suppose they must have passed on with their owners. Maybe other animals, like cows and sheep, had their own Other Lands to go to—the Baa-Moo-Quack-Snort-Grunt Lands or something. I wasn't very pleased, though, at not getting a proper answer.

"Can't you tell me how long I'll be dead for?" I ask. "I could be hanging around twiddling my thumbs forever. What am I supposed to do with myself? It doesn't seem very well organized here. In fact, this is all a bit of a dead loss."

"You can say that again," the man says, giving a shrug. "It's a dead loss, all right. That just about describes it." And he went back to his computer terminal, carrying on as if he were really different and important. Though as far as I could tell, he was as dead as the rest of us.

But I could see he wasn't going to give me an answer, no matter how long I stood there. So I walked off again, wondering what to do, and that was when I heard a voice call out, "Hello, there, maybe I can help you."

And that was how I met Arthur.

He was from another time, was Arthur. He wasn't dressed in modern clothes, but in old-fashioned ones. He looked like one of those boys out of those stories like *Oliver Twist* by Charles Dickens and all that.

Funnily enough, you seem to get to take your clothes with you when you die. And they never get dirty, either. They're always brand-spanking clean, like you've only just put them on. But are they clothes, I used to wonder, or just the *memory* of clothes? Same as you haven't really got a body anymore, just a *memory* of a body. And that's maybe all we really are, all us dead people, just a whole lot of memories, all walking about.

Arthur's clothes still managed to look pretty scruffy, though, even if they were spotless. And they were certainly pretty ragged and patched all over with odd bits and pieces. And he wore a hat—which is very unusual for a boy. I don't mean a baseball cap, but a proper big top hat, like undertakers wear in the drawings of old funerals. And that's what Arthur was—or used to be—or still is—or whatever tense is right. It gets very confusing, being dead. All your "was"es and "is"es and "used to be"s don't really seem to apply anymore, and you don't know your "are"s from your "were"s.

Anyway, Arthur must have been a good hundred and fifty years old as the crow flies, I reckon, but he didn't show his age a bit. He was pretty agile and very good at somersaults, and he had this neat trick where he used to stand on his head with his top hat still on. He used to look like some kind of little Santa Claus then, stuck head-first down a chimney.

It turned out that Arthur had been exactly the same age as me when he'd died, all those years ago. But he hadn't aged a day since. Time's different here in the Other Lands—people don't get any older. They stay at the age they were when they died. I don't know if time even passes at all here, not like it did back home.

When I asked Arthur if he'd been knocked over by a truck as well, he said, no, he'd died of some kind of fever. He said children his age were always dying of fevers back in the olden times, and that if you kept your eyes peeled you'd see loads of boys and girls about, walking around in old-fashioned costumes, and they were all dead of fevers, just like him.

I asked him if it hurt a lot, dying of fevers, and he said it did a bit to start with, but once it got really bad, you sort of passed out cold, and the next thing you knew you were dead. And that was it. And you didn't have the fevers anymore.

So I asked him then how he came to have his top hat with him. Because why would he be wearing his top hat if he was lying in bed with the fevers? But he said that he wasn't in bed. He was sleeping in the stable with the horse. And I said, What horse was that? And he said that it was the undertaker's horse. And so I asked him then why he wasn't wearing any pajamas. And he said that back in those days horses didn't wear pajamas. So I said, no, no, I mean why weren't *you* wearing pajamas, when you were ill with the fevers. And Arthur said that just like the horse, he didn't have any pajamas, either. The only clothes he had were the ones I could see him standing up in, and he had to keep his hat on because of the drafts. The ones in the stable, that is.

He seemed to get annoyed with me then for asking so many questions and we nearly had a bit of a row about it. But it soon fizzled out, and I must admit that it did seem pretty daft having an argument with a dead person. So Arthur and I made up and promised not to quarrel.

I asked him then why he'd been sleeping in the stable, and he said that's how it was for some children in those days, a stable was the best you got. And I thought that must have been a bit rough. Because when we went on holiday once, I had to share a bed with my sister, and that was bad enough. But sharing a bed with a horse must be even worse. Though, then again, if I had to choose between spending the night with my sister and spending the night with a horse, I might well choose the horse, because I couldn't see it snoring as much as she did, even if it did whinny a bit. And it certainly couldn't have made worse smells. At least, that's my opinion.

So I told Arthur this and asked him what he thought, but he said that having not met my sister, he wouldn't care to speculate on the matter, and that if you couldn't say anything good about people, you maybe shouldn't say anything at all.

I said to Arthur that if he waited long enough, he probably would get to meet my sister, because she'd be bound to die eventually, same as everyone else, and then he'd be able to decide for himself. He pointed out, though, that she might be an old woman by then. And that made me feel very strange, to think of my sister being an old, old lady, and me still a boy, and us meeting again one day, and feeling awkward and not really knowing what to say.

Talking about dead people, I asked Arthur where his mum and dad were, but he said he'd never been able to find them, though he'd looked for years. The trouble was that his mum had died in childbirth, and so he'd never really known her. He said a lot of mothers died while having babies back in those days.

So I said, What about your dad, then? But he'd never really known his dad, either, and he'd been brought up in the workhouse, just like Oliver in the Charles Dickens story. And then he'd ended up as an undertaker's boy, also just like Oliver. In fact, I started to wonder if he *was* Oliver, or maybe the model for him. But when I asked him, he'd never heard of Oliver, or of Charles Dickens, either. And I suppose the difference was that Oliver sort of got rescued in the end and went on to live happily ever after. But Arthur didn't. He got the fevers and died in the stable, lying next to the horse with no pajamas and wearing his battered top hat. And I thought about baby Jesus then, and how he was born in a stable. And here was Arthur, and he'd gone and died in one. And I thought that was a bit of a coincidence, really, in its own way.

I suggested to Arthur that maybe he could try and track his mum down. I thought that maybe the man on the Desk could help him, and look her up on the computer. But Arthur said he'd tried that and it was hopeless, because the man on the Desk didn't have any sort of a proper filing system at all and his computer skills were next to useless. Besides, he was all on his own there, trying to check everyone in, and as you can imagine, there were loads and loads of people, all trying to find their relatives, and it could be real chaos sometimes.

There were loads of people going round the Other Lands looking for their long-lost nearest and dearest, but in Arthur's case it was made so much worse by the fact that he didn't even know what his mum looked like. So in a case like that, where do you even start? I mean, talk about needles in haystacks. It was quite a job he had there, and I told him as much.

"I hate to say it, Arthur," I told him, "but I can't see you finding her easily. Especially when you don't even have a photo or anything, or a little picture in a locket, like you're supposed to have. You should definitely have a photo in a locket, at the very least. That's the minimum requirement, just to get your system up and running. You definitely slipped up there, Arthur, not having one of them."

He sighed then and said, "I don't even have a *locket*, Harry, mate. Never mind one with a *picture* in it. All I have is this."

And he showed me this little ghostly button he had, which he said he'd had since he was a baby, and which was supposed to be off his mother's blouse. He didn't know if it was true or not, but it was what he'd been told by the people at the workhouse. But, then, you never know, do you? Maybe it was all lies. Maybe it was just any old button and they'd just given it to him to shut him up and because they felt sorry for him, and so he'd have something as a keepsake, even if it wasn't a real keepsake at all.

He handed me the button to look at. It was sort of coated in seashell—mother-of-pearl, I think it's called. It was a nice button, almost like a piece of jewelry. I admired it and then gave it back to him, and he put it away carefully in one of his ghostly pockets.

"I'll tell you one thing, though," Arthur says to me. "I'm not going till I find her."

He surprised me a bit, saying that. I looked at him, sort of puzzled. "Not going *where*, Arthur?" I asked. "Where *is* there to go? We're dead, aren't we? This is it. Where else is there to go now?"

Arthur looked at me then as if I was dead ignorant.

"How long have you been dead exactly, Harry?" he says.

"I dunno," I said. "I'm not really sure. Not that long. It feels like I've only just arrived."

"Oh," he said. "That explains it, then. You wouldn't have heard."

"Heard what?"

"I mean, they wouldn't have told you."

"Told me what?"

"You have to find out everything for yourself here, Harry," Arthur said. "You'd think they'd give you a proper book on it. Not just that useless leaflet."

"But I don't understand, Arthur," I said. "Where is there to go? Where can you go when you're dead? It's the end of the line, isn't it?"

"No, there's more to it than that," Arthur said. "The next step is the Great Blue Yonder."

"Great Blue what?" I said, thinking the name rang a bell somewhere.

"Yonder," he said. "Over there."

And he pointed toward the far horizon, where the sun was always setting but never quite did, and where, behind all the reds and golds, you could just about make out a faint haze of blue.

And I remembered that the Great Blue Yonder was mentioned in the leaflet, too.

"What happens there?" I asked.

"Well, you know," he said, "you make your way there when you feel ready. You can go for, well, you know— what do they call it?"

"I don't know," I said. "I'm the new boy here. What *do* they call it?"

"You know," he said. "Thingamajig. Whatchamacallit. Thing."

"Thing?"

"Yeah, you know. It's like the next step, when you're ready. They've got a new name for it now. Oh, what is it? It's here on the tip of my-my—"

"Tongue," I said helpfully.

"I've got it," he said. "Recycling! That's what it's called now. Recycling."

I looked at him, puzzled and surprised.

"Recycling?" I said. "What's that mean?"

15

"I'll tell you about it later," he said. "I think I just saw someone who might be my mum."

And he went.

"One thing, though, Harry," he called back to me, "in answer to your question—"

"What question?"

"About how long you're dead for?"

"Yeah?"

"It depends."

"Depends?"

"On how long you want to be dead for. It all depends on you. I'll see you later. Don't go too far away. I'll find you. Bye!"

And Arthur hurried away then, going off after this woman he'd seen who was dressed in an old-fashioned costume and carrying an old-fashioned umbrella that wasn't really an umbrella at all. That is, it was more to keep the sun off than the rain. A parasol is what I think they called them. She was wearing a bonnet, too. So she was obviously taking no chances; what with a bonnet *and* a parasol, she was ready for all sorts of weather.

Arthur ran after her, shouting, "Excuse me, excuse me!" with his pearly button held tightly in his hand, the button his mum had been wearing when she died. But when the woman turned to see who was calling to her, you could see that all the buttons on her blouse were in place and none of them were missing at all. So it wasn't Arthur's mum. Which was a shame, as she was a pretty lady, with a nice, kind face, the sort of lady you wouldn't mind having for a mum, if you could choose.

Arthur's face fell when he saw she had all her buttons

intact. "Oh, sorry," he said. "Sorry to bother you. I just thought you were someone I knew."

And the lady smiled kindly, and she touched him on the cheek with her ghostly finger, and her hands were clad in these elegant pale linen gloves.

"Sorry," she says. "I'm looking for someone myself." And she smiled her sweet smile, and was gone into the crowd.

I watched Arthur and saw how disappointed he was. It was almost as if he couldn't rest until he'd found his mum, as if he'd never be at peace with himself. It was almost—and this is going to sound very odd, but it's what I thought—almost as if he hadn't died properly. As if he still had unfinished business. And he wandered off into the crowd, too, looking for Victorian ladies with bonnets and parasols and a button missing from their clothes.

And I watched him go, and I thought that maybe I wasn't exactly at peace with myself, either, and that maybe I had a bit of unfinished business, too.

The Other Lands

Now, you might well be thinking to yourself that considering where I was (wherever *that* was) and in view of what had happened to me, that I'd be running into all sorts of people from way back when—all sorts of famous historical figures and such.

You'd expect—once you're dead—to meet all kinds of people from the past. You'd expect to see people from the Iron Age and the Stone Age and the Middle Ages, too. You might hope to run into somebody famous, like Napoleon, or Julius Caesar, or Charles Dickens or William Shakespeare, or the man who wrote *Winnie the Pooh* or anyone you care to name. And you might hope to get their autographs, or at least to exchange a few words and to tell them how famous they'd got over the years. Because they might not know, unless someone had already told them.

But no. Charles Dickens was nowhere to be seen. Attila the Hun was nowhere to be seen. People wearing animal skins, cavemen who'd died thousands of years ago, were nowhere to be seen. (Well, apart from Ug, but I'll tell you about him later.) Cleopatra was nowhere to be seen. Moses was nowhere to be seen. In fact, the overwhelming majority of dead people that you saw had all died—by the look of them—within the past few years. There were a few people like Arthur around, from a different era, but nowhere near as many as you might have thought. So where had they all gone? All the millions and millions of people who had died over the years, just like I had?

Maybe, I thought, they had gone to a better place. Just like they say on the gravestones in cemeteries—*Left This World and Gone to a Better Place.*

But it didn't seem better to me, just different.

So, anyway, there I am wandering around the Other Lands or whatever they're called, and I'm half-expecting to see all these famous figures from the past—or even a lot of ordinary people from the past, people you could have a chat with and compare things with. And you could tell them all about cars and jet planes and computers, and watch their jaws drop and their eyes go wide. But there are very few people like this around.

And even the ones who are from dim and distant times seem to have heard all about it already. And if you mention computers to them—even to Ug the Caveman—they just shrug, as if to say, "Yeah. Computers. So what?" and they go on their way. Not that Ug the Caveman says that. All he ever says is "Ug." So that's what we've ended up calling him, because even when you ask him what his name is, he just says "Ug" again, every time.

The people from the really olden times always seem to be searching for something, too. And they go on wandering and wandering, just as if there's something they have to find before they can die properly. As if they had unfinished business. Just like Arthur. And maybe, in a way, just like me.

Unfinished business. I suppose you could call it that. It made me feel bad, too, every time I thought about it. It was something I'd said to my sister, Eggy. Her real name was Eglantine, but I always called her Eggy, usually to annoy her. I think my mum and dad regretted calling her Eglantine, and had maybe done it in a moment of madness. Everyone called her Tina now, and she tried to keep Eglantine all hushed up, like it was a big embarrassment and an awful family secret and a big sort of skeleton in the cupboard that we were never to mention to strangers.

So everyone called her Tina, apart from me. And I stuck with Eggy, just to let her know that I had one over on her, no matter how posh she pretended to be to other people, and so as to remind her of her humble beginnings, before she got all swanky.

Anyway, we'd had this big row about her not letting me borrow her pens, just a few minutes before I stomped out of the house and rode off on my bike to buy my own pens from the stationer's with my pocket money. It was an awful, terrible, dreadful row, over nothing, really. And we'd said all the awful, terrible, dreadful things that brothers and sisters sometimes say to each other. And you mean them at the time, and yet you know you don't *really* mean them—you're just saying them because you're angry and upset.

Anyway, she wouldn't let me use her pens because she said I was too ham-fisted with them and used too much force and I always squashed the points of them and flattened her felt tips. So I ended up saying, Stuff your pens, then, I'll buy my own, and I wouldn't use your pens now if you paid me. I wouldn't even use your pens if you went down on your knees and begged me to a million times over.

And she said I could wait until the sun turned to ice— fat-face—before she'd do that! And I could go and buy my own pens, too, and good riddance to bad rubbish and she never wanted to see my ugly mug again, either. So just before I slammed the door, I said, Well, we'll see, we'll *see!* And I *hate* you! Absolutely hate you! And I hate this house and this whole family and I never want to come back or see any of you ever again. And she said, So don't, then. And I said, You'll be sorry. You'll be sorry you said that, Eggy. You'll be sorry one day when I'm dead. And she said, No, I won't be, *I'll be glad.* So get lost, and don't call me Eggy. And I slammed the door then, and I went off on my bike.

And got killed.

And now here I am, dead as mutton, as dead as a doornail. And the last terrible, awful words I said to my sister were, "You'll be sorry one day when I'm dead." And the last terrible, awful words she said to me were, "No, I won't be, *I'll be glad.*"

And I want to see her again so much. To say I'm sorry and that I didn't mean it. And so that she can say she's sorry, too, and that she didn't mean it, either. Because I know she didn't, anymore than I did. It was just one of those stupid things you say, and I know she must be feeling awful about it now, every bit as bad as me.

So I want to go back and to say that to her. To tell her that I love her, really, and that she's not to be sad, or to blame herself, or to cry, or anything like that. And to tell her that she can have all my stuff, including my special conker that's four years old now, and also my stick insect.

But I can't. I can't go back, can I? Because I'm dead.

So I think that I'm a bit like Arthur, and a bit like Ug the Caveman, too, probably. (Though who can guess what *his* unfinished business is? And he certainly can't tell us. All he can do is grunt and say "Ug" and look ferocious—when he's not looking stupid, that is.) But yes, I reckon that in some ways I'm like them both. I also have things to settle; I, too, still have things to do.

After Arthur had disappeared into the crowd, I wandered around a while on my own, thinking things over and trying to make some sense of them all. I gradually began to work it out then, little by little, and I slowly realized that being dead wasn't the be-all and end-all like you might think. Because if it was, then everyone would still be there in the Other Lands, wouldn't they? Everyone from time immemorial, everyone who had ever lived. But they weren't. So they must have moved on to other things. Maybe it all had something to do with the Great Blue Yonder, over there on the far horizon. And maybe I could move on, too. Or maybe I couldn't. Maybe it all depended on settling the unfinished business. Only how was I going to do *that?*

I walked around for a good long time, not really going anywhere in particular, just strolling aimlessly and nodding to the people I passed on the way.

What I said to Eggy those few minutes before the truck got me had been tormenting me ever since I'd arrived.

Of all the things to say, I kept thinking to myself. Of all the stupid things to say. Of all the final things there are in the world to say to someone, I had to go and say *that*—"You'll be sorry one day when I'm dead."

Because you sometimes imagine it, don't you—about being dead, and how everyone will be so upset, and they'll all cry something terrible, and they'll all be so sad as they carry your little coffin down to the cemetery, and everyone will say what a wonderful boy or what a wonderful girl you really were deep down inside—even if you were naughty occasionally and did have some nasty habits. Maybe it's just me, and maybe you've never done this, but sometimes I'd lie in bed at night, and just before I fell asleep I'd think what it would be like if I never woke up again, and what they'd all do and say, and how my mum and dad would break the bad news to everyone.

I'd imagine the funeral and the flowers and everyone at school being unable to believe it, and how anyone who had ever been nasty to me or said a bad word about me would feel really, really guilty. They'd feel really, really bad about it. And it would serve them right. But I'd find it in my heart to forgive them just the same. And Jelly

Donkins—who'd got me at the back of the gymnasium once—would really be sorry that he'd got me, especially now that he'd never be able to make amends for it. He'd feel bad for months, or even years, or even the rest of his life. And maybe he would start being kind to little children and sending money to Oxfam and helping old ladies cross the road and going on sponsored walks and doing good deeds every day—just to make it up to my memory. And all the grownups would be amazed, and they'd say, "Whatever has caused this change in a big, bad Jelly Donkins? Why, he seems like a different boy now. He's all but saintly. He's even stopped pulling the legs off spiders and shaking salt onto snails when his mum's not looking."

And no one would ever know why Jelly Donkins was a changed boy. Apart from me. Only I'd never tell anyone, because I'd be dead. But even dead, I'd still be an inspiration to others. An inspiration and a fine example.

One thing about these dreams I used to have, though, was that I was still there. I mean I was dead and gone, but I was also still there to see everyone, to see them find me all cold and peaceful in the morning, to hear them crying softly and tiptoeing about the house, saying things like, "Poor Harry, he was such a good, kind, marvelous boy" and "There'll never be another Harry, never."

And I'd feel really sorry for them, not having me with them anymore. And I'd wonder how they'd ever manage without me. And they'd probably have to go for counseling to get over it all, or drink some beer to drown their sorrows.

And to see everyone so sad about you dying—even if

only in your mind—it kind of made you feel all warm inside, just like you'd been sucking extra-strong peppermints. And you even felt a bit sort of heroic, too. Especially if you hadn't died in your bed, but more if you'd died from doing something brave like rescuing a little baby from a flooded river. And you'd just managed to swim to the riverbank with the baby in your arms and to return it to its weeping mother, who could never fully express her gratitude to you, as you collapsed and died right there in the mud. And they put a statue up in honor of your memory then, and they gave you a medal, even though you were dead, and couldn't wear it. And then all the local pigeons would come and stand on your head.

It was all right, though, that kind of stuff, all that imagining what it would be like when you'd gone. It did used to leave you sort of nicely sad. And no matter how upset the people you left behind felt, you yourself felt all serene and peaceful and faraway above it all. At least, that was how I pictured it. But that's not how it really is. Not when you have unfinished business. You feel quite bad yourself as well.

So, anyway there I was, strolling along through the Other Lands, admiring the scenery and wondering how those I'd left behind were getting on without me. I nodded to the other dead people I met and I went on thinking my thoughts, feeling bad about what I'd said to Eggy those few minutes before the truck had got me.

The people I met were all very nice, in general—apart from Ug the Caveman. I said hello to him, and all he said back was "Ug." But, then, that's all he ever says to anyone, and he probably doesn't really know any better. So I nodded to them all, and they all nodded back to me, and we strolled along on our way.

"Hello," you'd say.

"Hello," they'd reply—if they spoke the same language. If not, they'd just wave and smile.

Yes, they're quite a friendly bunch, really, all the dead people. Which is quite extraordinary when you think about it. Because when I was alive, I used to be a big horror fan, and I was always reading these books about the slime coming up through the drain to get you, and about these ghastly apparitions from the underworld coming and grabbing you by the leg and dragging you down into the pit. And some of these books used to have titles like *The Gruesome Dead* and *The Cemetery Fiend* and *The Killer from the Creepy Coffin*.

But, really, people aren't like that at all. They're just ordinary, on the whole, and generally speaking they don't want to get you by the leg and drag you down into the pit—although there's maybe the odd exception. But most of them wouldn't even know what the pit was. And neither do I, come to that. Because I must have walked miles and miles, all over the Other Lands, and I never saw any pits anywhere. Just sort of trees and hedges and fields, like you'd see at home, with the odd bench where you can pause and admire the view.

But as for the gruesome dead and what-have-you, it's not like that at all. And if you don't believe me, well, you only have to think of your long-dead great-granny or somebody, who was probably a sweet old thing who wouldn't harm a fly. And she certainly wouldn't want to come back and get you by the leg and drag you into the pit. If she could come back in some way (which isn't altogether impossible, as I shall tell you about in a minute), it would probably only be to tell you to wrap up warm and not to forget your scarf. But you could hardly write a frightening horror story about that, could you?—about your great-granny coming back from beyond just to tell you to wrap up warm and to do your scarf up and to put your gloves on as it was nippy out. That wouldn't make much of a horror film, would it? Not that I reckon, anyway.

But I mustn't ramble. As I say, I was walking through the Other Lands wondering about the meaning of it all, wishing that I could just go back for a little while, just turn back the clock so that I could still be alive. I didn't want all my life back, only the last ten minutes of it. I just wanted to change what I'd said to Eggy, to alter it to, "Bye, Eggy, I love you" or "You've been a great sister, Eggy, even if we did fight a bit." Something nice. Or at least something that wasn't nasty. Even to say nothing—that would be something. Anything other than those awful last words, "You'll be sorry one day when I'm dead."

So I ambled on through the Other Lands, not really sure where I was going, not really sure if I was going anywhere. Because the Other Lands aren't quite like anything you see when you're alive. They're a bit like a walk through the country, like I said. Only there's no destination. No picnic sites. Nowhere to really get to. When you're alive and you go for a walk, you know that sooner or later the walk will come to an end. But the Other Lands aren't like that. The Other Lands are all journey and no destination. There's no real map, and yet you never get lost, but you never know

quite where you are, either. You can look for someone
and never find them—like Arthur and his mum. Or you
can not be looking for someone, and you meet them all
the time. And the only real place there is to get to is the
Great Blue Yonder. And yet my way never took me there—
as if I wasn't quite ready to go there yet.

So, anyway, there I am, strolling around wondering
what to do next, and I can't get Eggy or what I said to her
out of my mind. I don't know how long I've been walking—minutes, hours, days—but I decided to sit down on
one of the benches provided and admire the view of the
sunset, to watch that wonderful twilight, which never
quite turns into night.

As I sit down on the bench, I notice that there's a little ghostly brass plate on the back of it. Just like you get
when you're alive. Have you ever noticed? In parks and
places and at the seaside. When someone has died, their
relatives pay for a bench to be put somewhere for other
people to sit on. And there's a little brass plate on the
bench, which reads something like :

IN MEMORY OF GEORGINA
WHO ALWAYS LOVED THIS VIEW OF THE HILLS
(PRESENTED BY HER FAMILY)

Well, this bench I'm sitting on in the Other Lands had a
little plaque on it saying very much the same kind of thing:

IN MEMORY OF ALL THOSE
WHO LET GO AND MOVED ON
(PRESENTED BY THOSE WHO STILL WAIT AND LINGER)

And I start to wonder what "letting go" and "moving on" could mean and where all these people had moved on to. And it all seemed such a mystery.

So there I am, sitting on the bench on my own, when the next thing I know, I've got company. It's Arthur again, all top hat and patches.

"Wotcha," he says. "How are you doing?"

"Not so bad," I say. "Find your mum?"

"No," says Arthur. "Saw several who might have been her. But when I got a look up close, they had all their buttons. She'll be missing a button, see. I'm sure of it. I'm sure she's here somewhere and she's looking for me just as I'm looking for her. And I'll know her by the button missing, just as sure as she'll know me by having the button. In fact, that's the only way we *will* know each other, come to think."

"But, Arthur," I say to him, "what if she isn't here? What if she's—you know—moved on, whatever that means."

He gives me a funny look then. He almost seems a bit angry.

"No," he insists. "She wouldn't do that. Not without finding me first. No. She wouldn't. She'll be waiting and lingering, till she finds me."

"Yes, but suppose—" I begin.

"No," Arthur says, quite definite like. "She wouldn't. And I'm not letting go till I find her." And that seemed to be the end of the matter.

So I don't say any more. But I do wonder, about Arthur and his mum, and about me and Eggy, and about all the other people wandering around the Other Lands,

29

all looking as though they had things left undone. And I wonder again about the little plate on the back of the bench, that says *In Memory of All Those Who Let Go and Moved On*. And things begin to make a little bit of sense then. And I see that maybe the only way to move on is to settle your unfinished business, and then leave the past behind you, and then—

Well, then I'd just have to see.

Suddenly, Arthur leaps to his feet.

"Tell you what, mate," he says, and he has a bit of a twinkle in his eye and a bit of a grin on his face. "I know! Let's go and do some haunting!"

"Haunting?" I say.

"Yeah!" Arthur beams. "You can't be going round looking for people all the time! What's the point in being dead if you can't get a bit of fun out of it every now and again."

"But, Arthur," I say, "I'm not sure if you should—"

"'Course you should!" he says. "Come on, I'll show you how!"

And he starts moving on down the path.

"Yes, but—"

"Come on!"

"But I don't even know where to go—how to— I mean—are you saying you can—go back?"

Arthur stops and turns.

"'Course you can," he says. "You're not supposed to. But you can. It's easy once you know how. Come on."

I stand up, but I still hesitate. Going haunting, he'd said. I don't much want to go haunting. I don't like the idea of haunting at all. But going back. Well—yes.

Maybe I do want to go back. If only to see how they were all getting on without me and what had happened to the world—or at least the small part of it that I knew.

And yet still I hesitate. Arthur begins to get impatient.

"Come on if you're coming," he says. "Or I'll go without you."

But I still can't decide.

"Come on, Harry! What's to be afraid of? You're dead, aren't you? What can possibly happen to you now?"

"But, Arthur, if we go back—I mean—doesn't that mean—when we get there—as far as other people are concerned—we'll be ghosts?"

He laughs and grins and pushes his hat back so that it wobbles and nearly falls off his head.

"Ghosts!" he says. "Of course we'll be ghosts! What else could we be, Harry? We're dead, aren't we, after all."

"Yes," I say. "I suppose we are."

And I have to admit it, I don't have much choice. But it is one thing to be dead with all the other dead people, here in the Other Lands. But to be dead back in the Land of the Living—to be a ghost . . .

"I'm going, then," he says. "Are you coming with me, or aren't you? Last chance."

I hesitate still. He turns on his heel and makes as if to go. I suddenly think of Eggy, of Mum and Dad, of all my friends, of everyone who knew me. I suddenly and desperately want to see them all again. I can't live without them. Or even be dead without them. So in that split second I decide. I run after Arthur, calling as I go, "Hang on, Arthur, I'm coming with you."

And he stops and waits for me to catch up. Then we go headlong down the path. Back to the Land of the Living.

To the Land of the Living

Now, as a rule, I've never really been in favor of haunting or any of that kind of stuff, and I've never much liked practical jokes, either, as they all seem either cruel or silly.

It's not that I can't see the fun in it all—I can, up to a point. Creeping up behind people and going Boo! and that sort of thing, I'm sure it's all right in its way, and as long as you're in the right kind of mood there's no harm in it at all.

But you have to draw the line somewhere—at least, to my way of thinking—and it seems to me that all this haunting can get a bit stupid sometimes and totally out of hand.

I mean, say, for example, that you're on the sofa watching the telly or just daydreaming and your brother or sister or someone tiptoes up on you and goes *Boo!* right in your ear. Well, it gives you a bit of a start, doesn't it, and it can even make you all but jump right out of your skin—just like you were a snake.

So, anyway, when they do that, you might take it all in good part, or you might get a bit annoyed if you're not in the mood. So you quietly resolve to wait until *they're* daydreaming on the sofa and then you'll get them by bursting a paper bag next to their ear or by sticking a garden hose up their trousers and turning it on.

But on the whole, there's no harm done.

But just say that you were doing your homework when someone startled you. Or you were maybe trying to build a particularly difficult model airplane, and you'd just got to the really tricky bit when you suddenly get the boo in the ear. Total disaster. Seriously unfunny. They mess up your homework, they ruin your model, and it's not comical at all.

Well, a lot of haunting always seemed like that to me, at least the haunting you read about in books, with poltergeists breaking all the teacups and turning people's hair white and that kind of thing—stupid way to behave, if you ask me. I mean, what's the sense in it? It's all for no good reason. I don't see what's so funny about playing jokes on people and frightening them and making them look stupid. Seems to me you'd have to be pretty stupid yourself to even want to do things like that.

In fact, I always used to wonder about ghosts who did that sort of thing, hanging around old houses whispering in people's ears and making their hotwater bottles go flying out the window. I wondered if they'd maybe had a bad knock on the head at some point or they'd never grown up properly. Because, I mean, practical jokes aren't so bad when you're young and don't know any better, but when you're going on nine hundred years old or something, there's no

34

excuse. You ought to pack it in when you get to that age and take up something more sensible, like snooker or ten-pin bowling.

But, as I was to find out, it wasn't quite like that. Because a lot of haunting and going Boo! and frightening the living isn't just to do with practical jokes and having a laugh at someone else's expense. A lot of it is to do with all that unfinished business I was telling you about. And that's usually why houses get haunted and people get spooked—it's that unfinished business again. It's people like me, who, even though they are ghosts, seem to have ghosts of their own. And you might not think that ghosts could be haunted, but we can be, and some of us are. Haunted by the past. By the things we did and the things we said, by the things we never did say, by the things we meant to do but didn't.

So as Arthur and I hurried along through the Other Lands, him just a little bit in front, me trying to keep up with him, I did hope—for all he'd said about haunting—that he wasn't a practical joker. Because, as I say, I like a bit of fun and a good laugh as much as anyone, but practical jokes just turn me right off, as they always seem a bit cruel. I hoped I hadn't misjudged Arthur, that was all. But I was, no doubt, soon going to find out.

Arthur seemed to know the Other Lands like the back of his hand, and probably like the front of it, too. So he should, considering the time he'd spent there—over a hundred and fifty years, as measured in the Land of the Living. You'd think, though, after all that time, there wouldn't be any of it that he hadn't explored. And yet, as we hurried along the wide road that led back toward the

Desk, Arthur kept looking off to the left and right, and he'd spy new paths and new crossroads that he hadn't seen before. And he'd say, "I haven't tried that one yet. I must look down there," or "Maybe she's down along that way, maybe I'll find her today." And he'd take out the ghostly mother-of-pearl button from his pocket and rub it between his finger and his thumb, like he was rubbing it for luck. And you could tell he was thinking of his mum again, and wondering if he ever would see her.

I thought it was funny when he said, "Maybe I'll find her today," because there are no real *days* in the Other Lands, just that golden red glow of the sun that never quite manages to set, and the blue haze, shimmering away on the far horizon.

As we continued on our way toward the Desk, I realized that almost all the people we saw were walking in the opposite direction.

"We're going the wrong way, aren't we, Arthur?" I said.

"Nah," he said. "We're just going a different way to everyone else. That's not wrong. That's just different."

And I could see he had a point there.

I watched the other people stream by. They didn't seem like us, they didn't seem bothered with unfinished business; they seemed at peace and almost serene.

"Where're they off to, Arthur?" I asked. "Anywhere in particular?"

He looked at me as if I was a real ignoramus. But then he must have remembered that I was still a bit new at this being dead lark, and he shrugged and said, "The Great Blue Yonder, of course."

"Oh, yes," I said, trying to sound as if that explained

everything and I understood it all now. "Ah, right, yes. All off to the Great Blue Yonder. Right, Arthur. OK." Though I didn't really know what he was talking about or what that meant.

But I wanted to find out, I really did. In fact, I'm on my way to do that right now, just as I'm telling you this—well, thinking about it—hoping someone will hear.

That's maybe the only way I can describe it, really. It's a sort of thinking. Like thinking to yourself, but sort of broadcasting your thoughts out, too, the way a radio station sends out a signal—and I'm hoping that someone out there will have the right kind of receiver to pick me up.

Since being dead, I've had a lot of thinking time, and a lot of thoughts to fill it with. I've thought a lot about being alive, and about all the things I used to just accept and take for granted. Things I didn't think were strange in any way. But now I'm not so sure.

Take books and stories, for example, and where they come from. Take the way people who tell stories say, "I had an idea. I suddenly had a great idea. It just came to me from nowhere, just like that. It was a gift. The story wrote itself."

That's what they say somctimes. And I'm sure that's right. I'm sure that's what they honestly believe—that it "just came from nowhere."

But it can't just come from *nowhere*, can it? Only *nothing* can come from *nowhere*. *Something* has to come from *somewhere*. And I think that sometimes ideas come from people like me, over here in the Other Lands. From people like me with a story to tell but who aren't really able to tell it for themselves anymore, as they don't have the hands to hold a pen, or the fingers to tap at a keyboard.

They need someone to tell their stories *for* them. So we kind of send them out—broadcast them, if you like— to someone who has the patience to listen. And that person might be a lady or it might be a man or it might be a girl or a boy. I don't know. And I don't think it matters. What matters is what you have to say.

That's something I always wanted to know about when I was alive. Why, if ghosts ever came back with a message for anyone, it would only be to say that "Uncle Norman sends his best," or "Great-Auntie Beryl says all is forgiven and to remember to feed the budgie." Because you don't want to hear about that sort of stuff, do you? If a ghost is going to come back and say something, why doesn't it tell you what it's like to be dead? Why do they never mention the Other Lands, and the man at the Desk, and the sun that never quite sets, and the Great Blue Yonder?

You know, sometimes I think that these spiritualists and clairvoyants and astrologers are simply making the whole thing up.

Arthur and I got nearer to the Desk and to the path that led back down to where we had come from—the Land of the Living. The long queue for the Desk was still there, longer than ever, and the man at the Desk looked as miserable as ever and as bored as ever, too.

"Name!" he'd say as each new person came along. "Address. Contact number in case of emergencies."

"What do you mean, contact number for emergencies?" the woman in front of his desk said. "I'm dead, aren't I? I've already *had* my emergency."

38

The man at the Desk peered at her.

"Rules," he said, "is rules. And paperwork is paperwork. And computers—apparently—is computers."

"Then they're pretty stupid rules, aren't they?" the woman said. "And it's pretty stupid paperwork as well. And they're pretty stupid computers."

"Look, I don't make the rules, I just enforce 'em," the man at the Desk said.

"Then you're a blithering idiot," the lady said. She looked a bit to me like she might well have been a schoolteacher or a headmistress when she was alive.

"Now, see here, madam—" the man at the Desk began.

But I didn't hear anymore of the conversation because . . . *"Now!"* Arthur hissed at me. "While he's distracted. Come on!"

And so saying, he began to run, and I ran after him, and the two of us dodged past the woman and past the Desk and we raced on down along by the queue of people waiting to come in.

The man at the Desk must have seen us, though, because I heard him shouting from behind.

"Oi! You two! You boys! Where do you think you're off to? You're going the wrong way! Come back!"

But we paid no heed to him and ran on.

"Come on," said Arthur. "Come on, Harry. Don't worry. He can't come after us. He's not allowed to leave his desk."

"Stop them!" the man at the Desk shouted. "You in the queue there, stop those boys."

But no one even tried to. They were all too dazed and bewildered and unfamiliar with it all. They looked at us with a sort of confused surprise. But they didn't attempt to stop us. And why would they? Some of them could have been dead no more than a couple of minutes, and it does take you aback a bit for a moment or two, to work out what's going on.

You know what you think when you first realize you're dead? The thoughts that run through your mind? Well, first you think, "Where am I?" Then you look about and you see you're in the queue leading up to the Desk, and you somehow instantly know that you're dead. You know it, just like that. Just like you used to know whether you were hungry or thirsty or not. It's that simple.

Some people are too dazed to get the hang of it immediately, and they stand there saying, "Where am I? What happened?" But usually someone else in the queue will come to their rescue and explain.

"You're dead, mate," they'll say. "You've had your chips. You've done your time and it's over. But don't worry about it, we're all dead here. We're all in the same boat."

And that's when you go into the second stage—the stage of not believing it. That's when you think, "*Dead? Me?* No. I can't be, surely. I never finished my homework," or "I never put the cat out," or "What's going to happen to all the money in my piggy bank?"

Though, why you should worry about your money is totally daft. Because you know that expression "You can't take it with you"? People often say that, don't they? "Money—it's not everything. Put some by for a rainy day, of course, but what's the sense in hoarding it? You can't take it with you."

But that's only half the story. The point isn't just that you can't *take* it with you. The point is that even if you *could*, there'd be nothing to *spend* it on when you got there. Because there aren't many shops here. None, in fact. None at all.

Anyway, that's stage two: "Me? Dead? I can't believe it." Then stage three is getting used to the idea, and stage four is just moping about for a while, thinking about your life and sort of saying goodbye to everyone inside your own mind. Then once you've done that and when you feel at peace, you seem to make your way to the Great Blue Yonder.

But sometimes people get stuck between stages. People like me and Arthur and Ug the caveman, who can't move on because something's holding them back. Because they've got that unfinished business I was telling you about. And that's what it all comes down to—unfinished business—in the end.

So we ran on down past the line of people queuing to check in at the Desk.

"Oi! Oi!" the man at the Desk shouted again. "Come back here! Don't you go nipping back down and causing any mischief. Oi! You two! It's you two boys I mean!"

But we were gone by then, out of sight, if not yet out of earshot, and there was no way he could fetch us back.

Arthur was in front of me. The tails of his old-fashioned coat were flapping as he ran and he held his hat on with both hands, clutching it by the brim. It was a funny way to run, but it didn't slow him down any, and it was all I could manage to keep up with him. In fact, we were going so fast that I didn't see the precipice. He hadn't

41

warned me about that. One second, there we were, running helter-skelter, pelting down past the queue up to the Desk; the next we'd rounded a corner, and suddenly there was nothing there. And I mean *nothing*. Absolutely nothing. Not nothing like you know it when you're alive. Not nothing like in "nothing doing" or "nothing much on the telly," but absolute total *nothing*. Just a cliff and beyond it—nothing. No light, no darkness, just . . . nothing.

But it was too late to stop. Too late to even try. We just ran around the corner, stepped out into the void, and then suddenly there we were, falling through vast regions of nothingness, and I started to scream at the top of my voice.

"Help!" I yelled. "Help, help! Somebody help! I'm going to die!"

That's right. I *know*. I *know* it was stupid. But I've got to admit it, it's what I said. "Help, help! I'm going to die!"

And it never occurred to me that I *couldn't* die, on account of being dead already. So there are advantages to being dead, you see. It's not all bad news. At least, you only have to do it the once. It's not like having a wash or having injections or doing your piano practice, which you have to do over and over. You only need to die the once and then you needn't bother with it ever again. So, in a way, it's a big load off your mind.

"Help!" I screamed again. "Help! Arthur! Help!" And I closed my eyes and waited for whatever was down there to hit me.

For a second there was absolute silence. Not even the sounds of falling or the whistling of the wind. And then I seemed to hear the sound of laughter.

I was still too afraid to open both my eyes, but I managed to half open one of them. It couldn't be much longer, I thought—any second now I'd go splat on something. A very big, loud, and painful splat, too. And I didn't remember that nothing could hurt me, not anymore.

And there was the laughter again. Only it wasn't what I'd first thought. It wasn't the baying, cackling, malicious laughter of demons. We hadn't jumped into some great pit of hell and damnation, as I was starting to fear. No. It was the laughter of sheer delight. It was Arthur's laughter. And he was laughing for the joy of being—well, dead, I suppose.

And I realized then that we weren't falling at all.

We were flying.

And the earth that I had once lived on was down there, far beneath us, and we were flying above it, free as birds, and it was the greatest feeling ever. The greatest feeling in the whole wide world.

Back Down

It's a funny old world when you see it for the first time, and you know something? You never really do until you're dead.

You might *think* you do, and I'm sure you could cite me instances and say, "What about *babies,* then? *They* see the world as new, don't they? They see it all as fresh and different the first time they open their eyes." But they don't, you know, not really, because they can't understand it, they don't know what it is. They just see eyes and faces and hear people going, "Ooos a dittle didums den!" and "Coochie, coochie, coo!" and it doesn't make any sense at all.

When you're only about half a minute old, you've no idea what a face is or what a nice bit of scenery might be, let alone a crib or a nappy. And as for what a "didums" is and what a "Coochie, coochie, coo" might be, you're totally lost.

Anyway, what I'm trying to say is that you never really

get to see the world as it actually is. Not as if you'd just arrived in a flying saucer. Not as a totally brand-new place, as if it had crept up on you at once, and *boom!* there it was—the planet Earth.

So it was quite a sight to see, as Arthur and I swept down upon on it, swooping lower and lower, like great birds of prey flying down from high mountains to the lowlands.

Yet, even as we flew, I felt sort of once-removed— if you understand what I mean. A bit like they say about relations, like when you have a cousin once-removed, meaning sort of distant and faraway. It was as if you were part of what was all around you and you could see everything that was happening, yet you had no way of influencing events. You were like a goldfish in a bowl, watching the world outside.

We flew on down through the clouds.

"It's great, Arthur!" I shouted. And by the way of an answer, he looped the loop. So I had a go, and I got the hang of it at once.

"What way?" I called to him.

"Just follow me down," he said. "We'll go all the way."

So down we went. And as we did, I started to recognize many old familiar landmarks. The spires of churches, the tops of high buildings, fields with pylons in them, and then the flashing neon lights of the billboards, lights which stayed on all day but which only really came alive at night.

And somehow that sort of described Arthur and me— alive at night. And I thought, That's what I am now, one of those creatures of the darkness you're always reading

about in horror books. And I thought, Fancy that! What a
turn-up. Fancy harmless old me being a scary creature of
the darkness. And it sort of made you smile, really, and
feel a bit pleased with yourself, and it made you wonder
if people had ever got anything right. Because how was
I ever going to frighten anyone? *Me!* Who'd hardly say
boo to a goose, or to a duck, or to a turkey, or anything.

We swooped down over the city. The traffic roared
beneath us, but with a muffled, muted roar, as if behind
a pane of thick glass. That's how it all was, the real world.
It was shielded from us behind an invisible barrier, and
we could watch, but we couldn't take part anymore. We
couldn't do anything, or make anything happen. Or at
least that was what I thought. But on that count, I'd got
things a bit wrong.

"This way," Arthur shouted. "We'll go jackpotting."

"Jackpotting?" I called after him. "What's that?"

"You'll see," he said. "Come on."

On he flew, and I flew after him. We were level with
the buildings now, flying past the top stories of the high
office towers and the big hotels and the great department
stores.

"Wotcha!" Arthur shouted as we flew by a window.
There was a man inside, sitting alone at a great big desk,
which was so huge that you could have played table ten-
nis on it or even have had a game of five-a-side football
at a pinch. He looked like he was really important, with
his great big desk and his great big office—though, to tell
you the truth, he was doing something a bit nasty,
because he was sitting there with his finger up his nose.
Yes, that's what I thought—disgusting.

Anyway, Arthur swooped over to the window and looked inside the room.

"Ya!" he yelled. "Wotcha, baldie!" he called—because the man was going thin on top. "We can see what you're doing!"

And he pulled the most horrible face I've ever seen anyone pull. And I've seen some bad ones, believe me, because we used to hold competitions at our school for who could look the ugliest. And I quite often used to win.

"Hey, wooden brains!" Arthur called. "Where's your manners!" And he put his thumb to his nose and waggled his fingers. But the man just carried on as though we weren't there—which we plainly weren't, as far as he was concerned. And then there was a knock at the door, and he pretended to be busy with some paperwork, and he shouted, "Come in," and another man entered with some papers for him to sign. So he signed the papers and looked important for a while, and then, when the other man had gone, he began to draw doodles on his notepad. Doodles and matchstick men, just like you'd do yourself when you were bored. So maybe he wasn't so important after all, not if all he had to do was to sign papers and do doodles and wait for five o'clock to come round so that he could go home.

"He can't see us, Arthur," I said as we gawped in.

"'Course not," he said. "We're ghosts, aren't we? You don't see ghosts, do you? Come on, let's go and do some jackpotting. This way."

We were just about to fly on when a voice called from behind me.

"Hello, boys," it said. "How are you?"

47

I turned, and there was a woman, quite a beautiful one, flying along behind us. She looked quite young and quite modern. Not as modern as me, but not as old as Arthur. More sort of in between. Pretty recent, anyway.

"Hello, Miss Truly," Arthur said. "Keeping well?"

"Not so bad, Arthur," she said. "Mustn't grumble. There're plenty worse off than me."

I couldn't quite imagine who she meant, but I didn't say anything, and I just watched as she flew off down toward one of the windows of the cathedral and popped inside.

"Who was that?" I asked Arthur.

"Miss Truly," he said.

"Miss Truly who?"

"Don't know. Just Miss Truly, as far as I know."

"What unfinished business has she got?" I asked him.

"Don't know," he said. "Something to do with true love, I should think. It's mostly true love," he said, "is unfinished business, one way or another. Come on."

He swooped down toward the street then, and I followed along behind him. He turned a corner and nipped into a place called the Golden Arcade—Hottest Slots in Town—the kind of place my mum always told me I wasn't to go into, as they were a waste of time and money.

We went inside and Arthur peered around, looking to see who—if anyone—was playing the one-armed bandits.

An old man was in there on his own, feeding coins from a paper cup into a machine with lots of flashing lights on it. The old man looked a bit lonely, as if the slot machine he was playing on was his only friend. The fruit machine promised no end of "Big Wins" and "Huge Jackpots," and although the old man looked as if he could have done with a big win and a jackpot to pad out his pension, it didn't seem as though he'd had one in a long time.

He needed a row of four strawberries to get the big prize, and the odds were plainly stacked against him. We watched as he dropped his last coin into the slot and reached out to pull the handle.

"Now watch this," Arthur said.

Arthur stared at the fruit machine, at the rotating drums as they spun around. He stared at them intently, his face kind of screwed up a bit, as if he was concentrating really hard and focusing all his thoughts upon the little strawberries and oranges and coconuts as they went round and round.

Scrunch!

One of the drums stopped. On a strawberry.

Arthur smiled, then concentrated hard once more.

Click!

The next drum stopped. A strawberry again.

The old man watched, bleary-eyed, with no real hope or expectation of winning. He'd plainly had two strawberries before, but it had never come to anything.

Scrunch! Click!

Another strawberry—three now.

Scrunch!

The last one. Four. Four strawberries in a row! There was a pause, a lull, a moment's silence, then the slot machine shuddered and seemed to give an enormous hiccup before belching out a great cascade of coins. They tumbled out into the slot tray and spilled over onto the floor.

The old man pounced on them with delight.

"I've won!" he shouted. "The jackpot! I've won!"

The manager of the amusement arcade smiled thinly at him from his stool behind the change booth and did his best to congratulate him. But you could tell that he was miffed, really, that the old man had won.

The old man gathered up his winnings and stuffed the coins into his pockets until they bulged almost fit to burst.

He looked as if he were on his way out then, to celebrate his winnings with a pint of beer and a pork pie in the pub.

But as he headed for the door, he paused and dropped a coin into another machine.

"Just for luck," he said.

I saw Arthur furrow his brow, stare at the machine, and start to concentrate again.

This machine was a little different. You didn't want strawberries to win on this one, but a row of silver stars. The old man pressed the start button.

Clunkity-click, clunkity-click, clunkity-click, clunkity-click.

And there they were, four sliver stars in a row. And another mass of coins was dropping from the machine. The old man practically danced for joy. He had to borrow a carrier bag to put all his winnings in. But the arcade owner just looked furious, and he hurried the old man out of the door before he could play on any other machines or win anything else.

"Early closing!" he said. "Sorry."

"But I'm feeling lucky today," the old man protested, "I'm on a winning streak, I can't stop now."

"Then you'll just have to go and be lucky somewhere else," the manager said. "You can't be lucky here anymore. I can't afford it."

He closed the door and locked it and turned the sign round in the window.

I looked at Arthur and saw that he was laughing. And as far as I could tell, he had done it all.

"Arthur!" I hissed across at him, in a kind of harsh whisper, forgetting that nobody would be able to hear me, apart from another ghost. "Arthur! Did you do all that?"

"Of course," he said. "It's easy enough when you put your mind to it."

The arcade manager meanwhile was taking the back off the strawberry fruit machine and tinkering inside with a screwdriver.

"What happened there?" he muttered. "How did he win the jackpot? That's not supposed to happen."

"Arthur," I said, "don't you think we should get out of here before it all turns nasty?"

"Oh, he won't know it was me," Arthur said. "He'll just think it was one of those things. You know, like a gremlin in the works."

Arthur was certainly that, all right.

But it was hard to have any sympathy for the arcade manager. It served him right, really. All my sympathy was with the old man.

Arthur walked out through the closed door, just like the ghost he was. And I followed him out to the street.

"Where to, then, Harry?" he said. "Where do you want to go? Anywhere you fancy in particular?"

I suddenly had an idea then. I suppose it was inevitable in a way. I was bound to think of it sooner or later. And it was such a temptation that who could resist it? Nobody I knew. And I bet you wouldn't have been able to, either.

"Tell you what, Arthur," I said. "Let's go and have a look at my house. See how my mum and dad are, and Eggy, and Alt the cat and—"

But Arthur didn't look very happy about that idea.

"I dunno, Harry," he said. "I dunno if I'd recommend you to do that. See, that's what I did, you know, the first time I went haunting. I went off looking at all the old faces and the old places—"

"We can go round to my old school, too, Arthur!" I said. "I'll show you my class. And my seat in the classroom. I bet they'll have kept it just as it was, Arthur—only it'll be all decorated now with flowers and mementos and things. I bet it will."

"Harry—" he tried to interrupt me, but I was well away then, and I wouldn't listen.

"Yeah!" I continued. "Come and see my house, Arthur, and my family, and my old school. And I'll show you the park where I go—I mean, where I *used* to go—on the weekends for football and stuff. And I can show you where I used to ride my bike. And I'll show you where the accident happened. And the local swimming pool, too, Arthur, where I used to go swimming and—"

"No, Harry," he said. "I'm not so sure about that—"

But there was no stopping me then, no stopping me at all.

"Yeah, Arthur," I said. "Let's go! Let's go now. I'll introduce you to Eggy, my sister. Though that's not her real name. She's called Eglantine, really, which is a flower's name—or at least a plant or something. You'll like her. She's all right. I mean, we argue a bit, but then brothers and sisters always do, don't they, Arthur—"

"Listen, Harry," he began to say, but I was well beyond listening to anyone. I'd made my mind up by then. My heart was set on it. I just *had* to see the old places, I just *had* to see my mum and dad and my sister again. And all my friends, too. I had to see how they were all managing without me. I had to, I just *had* to, no matter what.

"Come on, Arthur," I said. "Come on. Let's go to the school first!" Because I could see by the hands of the cathedral clock that there'd be no point in going home, as there wouldn't be anyone there yet. Eggy would be at her school (an all-girls one, and different from mine) and my mum and dad would both be at work, and nobody would be back at the house for hours.

"Harry, *wait!*" I heard Arthur cry as I sped off, heading for the north of the city and making for the patch of green that was the playing field of my school. "Wait up, Harry," he called. "It's not so simple. You've got to understand a few things first, Harry. You've got to understand. Wait up!"

But, as I say, I was past waiting up for anyone. My mind was decided, and once it's made up good and proper, it takes at least two earthquakes and a major hurricane to shift it.

"Wait up, Harry, wait for me!" he cried. But I sped on through the sky, past the buildings and over the traffic, skimming on the air the way a stone skims on water, skipping over the waves and foam.

"Wait up, Harry! Wait up! Wait up!"

But his voice faded far behind me, and I wasn't in the mood to wait up for anyone. Not even for the devil himself. And come to think of it, who *was* the devil? *Where* was the devil? Why hadn't I met him yet? Or was he just something else that didn't exist?

And you know what I thought then, as I sped along? I thought, There is no devil. Someone made him up once to blame things on and to frighten little children with. But there is no devil, not really, and the only devils that do exist are the ones you make for yourself. Devils and fears and worries and things that go boo and the monsters in the wardrobe, we usually make them up all on our own, without any help from anyone.

School

I hovered over the school gates and waited there for Arthur to catch up with me. He seemed to be taking his time, so I sat down on one of the great concrete globes that decorate the two pillars of the entrance. This wasn't because I was tired or anything—you don't really get tired when you're dead. Not even dead tired. And you don't get hungry or thirsty, either. Or anything, really. Nothing physical, anyway. But you still sort of have feelings, though. You can still feel happy or sad, or lonely even, or remorseful, or guilty. You can even laugh.

Anyway, I perched there on the concrete globe, not because I needed to rest but more for the look of the thing, really. Because it does look pretty cool, being able to perch on the top of the school gates, looking like you've been dead for centuries and it's all in a day's work. I suppose I wanted Arthur to see that I was really getting in to this being dead lark and that I'd got the hang of it already, and there was nothing to it, really.

As I sat there on top of the gates waiting for Arthur to get there, I started to wonder about the fruit machines and how he'd managed to control them, as if he'd done it with the force of his mind and nothing else. I wondered if I had those kinds of powers, too, and so decided to give it a go.

Just across the road from me was a large maple tree— one of those really big old ones that look as if they've been growing for years. It was getting so big it looked as if it might crack the pavement up with its roots, and the men from the council must have been round to crop its upper branches, because you could see where they'd recently been cut. And it may have been necessary, but it didn't look very nice. All in all, it looked like a tree that had just had a bad haircut and was maybe thinking about asking for its money back.

I realized, as I looked at the tree, that autumn must be setting in. Most of the leaves had fallen from it and had been trodden into a squashy mush on the pavement below.

I didn't think too much about this at first, but then the thought struck me that several weeks must have gone by since I had been done in by the truck. Because it had been late summer then—well, early autumn, I suppose, but with very summery weather. We'd only been back at school a couple of weeks when my accident happened. And now here we were—sorry, here *they* were—with winter nearly upon us—*them*.

It was odd that so much time had gone by. Because to me it seemed as if the accident had only just happened, no more than a few hours, or even a few minutes, ago. How could so many weeks have gone by without my noticing? How could so much time have vanished? So much would have happened that I'd have missed out on. They'd have started new projects at school. There'd be whole new games of football, and I wouldn't be on the team. They must be having a bad season, though, I was sure of that. Must be, when they were missing their best midfielder—yours truly. How could they ever have replaced me, I wondered? Maybe they hadn't been able to. Maybe they'd had to give up football altogether.

But then I heard the sound of people shouting and calling and kicking a ball around, coming from the field on the other side of the school. And I realized that football was still going on, even though I wasn't there. Still going on—without me.

I felt an odd sort of pang then. A pang of—I don't know—sadness, longing, of wanting—to be alive again, I suppose. But it soon passed, because I've always been the sort of person who tries to make the best of a bad job and look on the bright side. "What can't be cured must be endured," as they say. Or, in other words, "Like it or lump it." So I try to like it if I can, because who needs lumps, after all.

I turned my attention back to the tree. One of the upper branches had a solitary leaf left on it. Well, I thought, if Arthur can get four strawberries to line up on the fruit machine just by willing them to, there's no reason why I can't make that last leaf drop off just by doing the same.

So I started willing.

I stared at it, really hard, focusing my thoughts on it, the same way as you would focus the rays of the sun through a magnifying glass. And when you do that with a magnifying glass—as you'll know if you've ever tried it—you can focus the sunlight so sharply that the heat becomes intense and you can burn a hole in a piece of paper, or even a bit of wood, just by concentrating the sunlight on that particular spot.

"I'm the lens," I said to myself. "And my thoughts are the sunlight. And that leaf is the piece of paper."

So I stared and stared at it, trying not to move, to hold really steady—just as you need to keep the magnifying glass steady.

"Fall!" I thought. "Fall, fall, *fall!*"

But nothing happened.

I didn't give up, though, I kept on trying. Mind over matter, that's all it was. Because if Arthur could do it, why not me? I was as good as he was, and just as dead. The only difference between us was that he was maybe a bit deader. Or rather, he'd been dead longer. But just because you've been at something longer, that doesn't mean you're better at it. You may even be worse, because you've gone stale. Whereas if you're only just dead, you might have a whole new approach and a whole new way of seeing things and a fresh angle on it.

And besides, how *can* one person be deader than another? Because you don't really get the equivalent of good, better, and best for being dead, do you? Like, dead, deader, and deadest. I don't recollect doing that during English.

No, I was just as good and just as dead as he was. And besides, it's not really a competition, is it? You're just either dead or you're not. Same as you're either—I don't know—a kipper or you're not. You can't be half a kipper, can you? Or sort of a kipper. Or a kipper on Tuesdays, but the rest of the time you're a banana. And so that was what I thought. If Arthur could do it, why not me?

"Fall," I thought as I stared at the leaf. "Fall, fall! I command you to *fall*."

But the leaf clung on to that branch as if it had been Super-Glued on to it.

"Fall!" I went on thinking. "Fall, *fall!*" And I turned all my thoughts into a kind of small, tiny dot of concentration, and I aimed the dot of concentration right at that leaf, at exactly where it grew from the branch.

"Fall," I willed it. "Fall!"

And just then it began to move. It moved as if tugged at by a gust of wind. And I saw that the branch was swaying. It's true that it was quite a windy day, because you could see the clouds being blown about up in the sky, even if I couldn't feel the air itself on my face anymore, like I'd been able to back when I was alive.

It's a wonderful sensation, that, you know—the feel of a refreshing breeze on your face. I missed it. Funny how much you take for granted when you're alive, all the ordinary, simple things. But I missed it so much. More than I'd ever have thought. In fact, if I'd had to fill in a questionnaire when I was alive or write an essay called *Things I Will Miss the Most When I Am Dead,* I'd never have put the feel of the wind on my face in there. I'd have said things like my mum and dad, of course, and my friends, and my sister, even, I suppose, and all the things I'd got used to doing, and the football and the telly and the computer and all the rest.

But the wind on my face. I'd never have thought of that.

The leaf began to move, to tremble in the wind, making a sound like a piece of paper stuck in bicycle spokes.

"Fall!" I willed it. "Fall!"

It moved more rapidly. I don't rightly know if it was me doing it or if it was the gust of wind, or maybe it was a bit of both. But the leaf suddenly broke from the branch and fluttered down to the pavement, and it lay there on the ground, waiting for someone to tread on it and to turn it to mush like all the rest.

I felt a bit shocked, the way you do when you've just managed to do something you didn't think you could. Only *had* I done it? Had I? Or was it just the gust of wind? Maybe I ought to try it again on something else before—

But before I could there was someone calling my name.

"Wotcha, Harry. What you doing? Daydreaming? You look a bit far away."

I looked across, and there was Arthur, sitting on the opposite concrete globe on top of the other gatepost.

I blushed. Well, I would have blushed if I'd had anything left to blush with.

"Eh, nothing," I said. "I'm not doing anything. Just thinking."

Arthur hopped over from his gatepost and sat next to me on mine.

"Listen, Harry," he said. "I've got to tell you something. Got to warn you, that is."

"About what?" I said, only half listening to him, still looking around for another leaf to concentrate my great powers on.

"This your old school, is it?" Arthur said, jerking his thumb at the buildings behind me.

"That's right. Come in with me, Arthur," I suggested. "I'll show you about. I'll point out my class to you, and all my old friends and—"

"No, thanks," Arthur said. "I won't come in, if it's all the same to you."

"But, Arthur," I said, a bit annoyed and bewildered at his refusal, "it'll be really interesting. Things have changed an awful lot since when you were at school."

"Shouldn't think so," he said. "Not that much. Besides, I was never really at school much anyhow."

"No, but they have changed, really."

"No, I doubt it somehow. It's still reading, writing, and arithmetic mostly, I should imagine. We had that a hundred and fifty years ago. I shouldn't think much has changed."

"But, Arthur," I protested, "I can show you the computer room. I bet you never had computers."

"No," he conceded, "not the sort you have now. But we had some pretty good gadgets, you know. Mechanical more than electrical, but good just the same. And anyway, I've kept myself abreast of modern trends by popping down here to the Land of the Living every now and again to see how things were moving along. So I've seen computers already, thank you very much. It's no big deal to me. There's even one up in the Other Lands now, but it hasn't made much difference. They still can't find my mum."

I was rather disappointed at that, because I'd been looking on Arthur as a bit of a country cousin. The sort who comes up to the big city every once in a while with a straw stuck between his teeth and wearing big mucky wellingtons and who hasn't got a clue about anything except how to milk the cow. And you take him round the city and he keeps going, "Cor! I never saw anything like *that* before!" when you take him down to the bowling alley or round to the Laser Quest.

But Arthur didn't seem the sort to be impressed at all. I suppose he'd just seen too much already and had lived too long—well, you know what I mean.

"Anyway," Arthur went on, "to be honest, Harry, I'm not all that keen on school. I never went there much myself, and when I was there, I never liked it, as they used to whack us. I know they don't whack you these days, and you should consider yourselves lucky. But we got whacked all the time. And you can't really enjoy your schooldays, not when you're getting whacked. In fact, I don't think you can enjoy *anything* when you're getting whacked, because all you can think about is the whacking, and wonder when it's going to stop. And once it has stopped, you just worry if it's going to start again, and whether your bottom will ever get back to normal. So I'm not all that keen on schools, not really."

I stood up on top of the gatepost.

"OK, Arthur," I said. "Please yourself. I'll go in on my own. You can go back if you want to."

"No, I'll wait here," Arthur said, "until you've finished. You might not find your way back to the Other Lands on your own."

"I'm sure I can manage, thank you, Arthur," I said in a polite but distant voice, thinking to myself that if I could make leaves drop off trees, then I should be able to find my way back to wherever the Other Lands were without too much trouble.

"OK," he said. "Fair enough. I'll just hang on here a while anyway, just admire the scenery. You just don't want to get stuck here, that's all. A bit of haunting's all right for a laugh, but you don't want to get stuck here and have to do it forever."

"I'll be OK. Don't worry."

"OK," he said. "Well, I'll be here, anyway, for a while. If I've gone by the time you come back, I'll see you later."

"OK," I said, and I went to hop down from the gatepost and to make my way on into the school. I remembered then that he had been about to warn me of something a while earlier. He seemed to have forgotten it now. But that didn't matter. I wasn't bothered.

I jumped down to the ground.

Arthur peered down at me. He looked like an over-grown garden gnome up there in his top hat. All he needed was the fishing rod, and the picture would have been complete.

"Harry," he said, "don't expect too much, will you?"

"What?" I stopped and looked up at him.

"Don't expect too much—of other people. Life goes on, Harry. People are only human. So just don't expect too much. That's all. I went back myself once, you see, to have a look around, shortly after I got the fevers. I went and had a look round all my own haunts and stomping grounds, just to see how everyone might be getting on without me, how they'd be missing me and . . ." He

63

trailed off, and stared ahead, as if looking far back into the past.

"And *what,* Arthur?" I said. "And what, exactly?"

He looked down at me again and gave a faint smile.

"Just don't expect too much, Harry," he said. "And then you won't be disappointed."

I didn't know what he meant, really, but I couldn't be bothered to stay and ask him. I was impatient to get back into my old school and have a look around and see what kind of a difference my not being there had made.

I could hardly wait to see how they were getting on without me. Or rather *not* getting on without me. In fact, I wouldn't have been surprised if the whole place had ground to a halt. Because it wasn't just the football team that relied on me; I was quite an essential cog in the classroom, too. I was always one of the first with their hands up whenever there were any difficult questions. Not that I'm saying I always got the answers right—or that I *ever* got the answers right—but at least I'd have a go. But now that I wasn't there, who'd be keeping everything going? That's what I was dying to find out.

So I went on into the playground, to see how they were all coping without me. And as I did, the bell rang, and the doors flew wide open, and everyone burst out of the school—just as if it had erupted—for the morning break.

They all ran past me, all my friends and classmates. I think some of them might even have run *through* me. I got a bit excited and I think I must have called out their names.

"Terry! Dan! Donna! Simon! It's me, look, Harry, it's

me! I've come back on a visit. I've come back to see you! It's me!"

And then Jelly Donkins came out—big, fat, horrible, smelly Jelly Belly Donkins, who used to pick on me. He was carrying a plastic football under his arm, and he seemed like he might be trying to get a game up. Well, nobody would be playing with *him!* I could have told him that little simple fact and no worries. Nobody would be playing any football with Jelly Donkins. Not now that I was dead. Not when they all knew how he'd picked on me when I was alive. No one would ever play with him again, not ever. It would be like—what do you call it?— that's it—violating my memory.

I just hoped he felt bad about it, that was all. I really did. I just hoped he had a bad conscience that kept him awake at nights. And serve him right, too. I'd probably be there, preying on his conscience for the rest of his life, even when he was a big fat smelly old man, and for the rest of his death, too.

I put my tongue out at him. "Smelly Jelly Belly!" I jeered.

But he walked right past me, bouncing his football on the ground. Then he gave it a kick and ran after it, and disappeared into the throng of boys and girls.

Mr. Diamond was on playground duty. Out he came, as tall as ever, with his long droopy moustache.

"Hello, Mr. Diamond. It's me! Harry! How are you?"

But of course he couldn't see me or hear me. I knew that full well. I knew no one could see me or hear me. But that didn't stop me from crying out and shouting and waving like mad at everyone I knew.

And then Pete came out. Pete Salmas. My best mate. Well, bestest mate, really. We'd known each other for years and years. We'd been at the same nursery and then at the same school. Right back from the very beginning, from the very first class. And I can remember that so clearly, even now, years later. I can remember my mum leaving me behind, worried that I wasn't going to let her go quietly, that I was going to cling on to her and start to cry. But I didn't, because Pete was there, and he was the one friendly face among all that was unfamiliar.

We sat next to each other near the front of the class, me and Pete, we usually had our lunch together, and often both walked home from school.

"Hiya, Pete," I called—knowing that he couldn't hear me but wondering if perhaps I might still get through to him in some way. I mean, if I could get leaves to fall off trees, maybe I could somehow communicate with people who were still alive. Put thoughts into their minds, maybe. It might be possible.

"Turn round," I thought at him. "Turn round, Pete. I'm right behind you." And I thought at him as hard as I could.

But no. He didn't turn round.

So I went and stood beside him. He had his hands stuffed into his pockets, and he was staring out over the playground, as if looking for someone to talk to, someone to play with.

I knew that Pete would be missing me. If anyone missed me, it would be Pete. In fact, I'd have bet any money that it was me he was thinking of right then, even as he looked out over the playground. I'd have put any amount of pocket money on that.

"I'm here, Pete, right beside you."

But he just went on looking with that faraway look.

"It's Harry, Pete. It's me. Harry."

He shuffled his feet a bit. Took his hands out of his pockets, cupped them, blew into them to warm them up, then folded his arms so his hands were under his armpits.

We'd have been playing football usually, me and Pete. That was the routine for morning break. A bit of a kick-about, or maybe a game of handball or rounders. But there'd always be something. Even when it rained. We'd stay in class then and have a game of Battleships or Hangman or something like that. But there was always a game going on.

He'd be stuck now, poor Pete. You could see it. It made you feel a bit sorry for him, the way he didn't have anyone else, not like he'd had me. I was touched. I was, honest. He looked so on his own, and a bit lonely. Everyone else had their friends and their games, but Pete just seemed out of it, almost as out of it as I was. Except that he was still alive, of course, which made a big difference. So he just stood there, like a reserve on the touchline, waiting to be called onto the field of play. Only no one called him. And then—

"Hey, Pete!"

Pete looked up to see who was shouting to him. So did I.

"Pete! Pete Salmas!"

It was Jelly. Flipping Jelly Donkins.

Pete didn't answer. And I didn't blame him, either.

But Jelly called again. "Pete! Hey! Cloth ears!"

And that was typical of Jelly. He could never say anything really nice. Even when all he wanted was your attention, he still had to be a bit insulting about it.

"Whadda you want, Jelly?" Pete shouted back.

Jelly was about twenty feet away from him. He was bouncing his football on the ground with his hand, bouncing it like it was a basketball and he was just about to lob it through the hoop. Obviously nobody wanted to play with him. He was such an obnoxious pain in the neck, it was hardly surprising. You'd have to be pretty desperate to want to play football with Jelly Donkins.

Jelly stopped bouncing the ball. "Fancy a kickabout, Pete?" he said. "You up that end, me at the other?"

Pete didn't reply.

But I knew what he was thinking. I knew what was going through his mind, the same as was going through mine. The nerve of it, that's what he was thinking. The sheer *nerve* of Jelly Donkins, who'd been my sworn enemy all my days, and here he was now, trying to get all pally with my best mate Pete.

I just prayed that Pete didn't go over there and knock his teeth out, that was all. I mean, I knew he was capable of it, and I wouldn't really have blamed him if he had. I just didn't want him getting into trouble on my account, that was all.

Pete swallowed. Plainly trying to control himself and not let his anger and his indignation get the better of him. Then he swallowed again and he opened his mouth to speak, to tell Jelly Donkins what to do with his football. To tell him in no uncertain terms exactly where he could stick it.

I could hardly wait.

"OK, Jel, kick it over."

What? I had to be hearing things.

But no. Jelly had kicked the ball over and Pete was running toward it. And a moment later, they were off down the playground, and Jelly was trying to tackle Pete and to get the ball off him—which he did. And then Pete was after Jelly, and he got the ball again in his turn. Then he sprinted for the two trees that were the goalposts for break-time football.

Jelly ran to get into the goalmouth before Pete could score one, but Pete's shot rebounded off the tree trunk and it hit Jelly smack bang on the backside. But instead of getting all mad and huffy about it, like he usually did when things went against him, Jelly just sat down on the football and started to laugh. And then Pete started to laugh, and he went over and kicked the football out from under Jelly, and banged it between the posts. But Jelly just lay there on the ground, staring at the sky, going, "Ahhh! Ahhh!" and pretending to be a world-class footballer feigning injury. So you know what Pete did? He went over and *sat* on him, just like they were two good mates having a laugh. And instead of getting really mad, Jelly just *pretended* to get angry, and then Pete was off again with the football. And in a couple of minutes, there was a full five-a-side going on, and all sorts of people— who normally wouldn't have touched Jelly's football with a bargepole—were joining in. And all, in a way, because Pete had sort of given him the seal of approval.

And all I could do was to stand there, unable to believe it, my best mate and my sworn enemy, playing football together, and seeming to be enjoying it all. And me, barely cold in my grave. It didn't seem right, somehow. It didn't seem right at all.

I turned and looked toward the gates, to see if Arthur had been watching, and hoping that he hadn't. But he had, from his perfect viewpoint up on the gatepost, and he gave me a kind of sympathetic, almost pitying, look, as if he knew just what was going on. Though he couldn't have really, as I'd never told him that Pete was a special mate of mine, so how would he know?

I looked right through Arthur—not difficult, seeing he wasn't really there—and pretended I hadn't noticed him, and I turned back to watch the game.

It was hard to take, my best mate and my worst enemy getting on like the greatest of friends, just like they'd both forgotten all about me, just like I'd never even existed. I felt a bit disgusted with Pete, to be honest, and a bit betrayed by him, like he'd gone and done the dirty on me when I wasn't looking. Only I *was* looking, and I'd seen the whole thing.

I turned my back on the game and went wandering through the playground. I went over to the nature patch and looked for my earthworms in the old fish tank. But someone must have upended it, or maybe they had died, just like me, because the tank was clean and empty and my earthworms had gone.

I looked all over for traces of my old self. I looked for all the things I had left behind me that people might remember me by. I stood by the climbing frame and recalled how I was one of the first in our year to get to the very top of it and do a complete roly-poly around the top bar. But there was no means of knowing that now, and my famous roly-poly had vanished like mist in the morning.

I went round the playground, standing in between people who were having conversations, staring deep and questioningly into their eyes. Vanessa and Mikey and Tim and Clive—did any of them still think of me, did any of them remember? I even asked them outright. I shouted in their ears, yelled it to their faces.

"It's me!" I said. "It's *me!* Old Harry, come back on a visit. Don't you know me? Don't you remember me? Don't you know who I am?" And then most of all, "Don't you *miss* me?"

But the only person who could hear me was old-young, one-hundred-and-fifty-year-old Arthur, sitting perched up there on the concrete globe above the gatepost, with his top hat stuck on his head, looking at me with those awful kind and sympathetic eyes. Yet I still couldn't bear to meet his gaze. I couldn't accept his sympathy. What I wanted was some recognition from my old friends and classmates, the people I had played with and fought with and argued with and had gone to birthday parties with and on outings with and all the rest. Didn't *one* of them miss me? In a few short weeks, had they *all* forgotten me? Didn't *one* of them think of me still?

Well, it didn't look like it, and the playground games went on, just as they always had. And it seemed to me then that it was only the games that mattered, and as long as the games went on, it didn't really matter who played them, just as long as they went on forever.

It was creepy. Eerie. It spooked me a bit, even though I was a ghost.

But then I thought back to other children—Fran and Chas and Trevor—who'd all left to go on to different schools. And I remembered how I'd thought about them and missed them for a while. In fact, I'd even written a few letters to Chas at his new place, which was miles away. And he'd written back to me for a time, and he'd told me all about his new house and his new school and how they were getting on there.

But then writing the letters got to be a chore, and so I stopped writing to him. And he must have felt the same because he stopped sending anything to me. And then I gradually thought about him less and less, until finally I hardly thought of him—or Fran, or Trevor—ever at all. And then I realized I hadn't thought about a single one of them for ages. Not until today.

And maybe that was how it was for Pete. Maybe he'd missed me something terrible at first, and then, as every day went by, he thought of me less. And maybe that was only right. Maybe I'd have been the same, too. And it would have been pretty selfish of me to expect Pete not to ever have any other best mates for the rest of his life, and always to be on his own, just because I'd gone on.

I thought of Chas again and remembered something else—that although he was a friend of mine, Pete couldn't stand him. Just the same as I couldn't stand Jelly Donkins. But I'd never really asked Pete how he felt about Jelly; I just assumed he felt the same as me and didn't like him, either. But maybe he did. I'd not thought of that before.

So I suppose that was it, really—it was just like I'd gone on to another school, and little by little everyone would forget about me, and then one day no one would think of me at all. Not one of all the people I'd known. And it made me sad. It did.

I decided to give it one last go—one last go at trying to communicate. Maybe one of the teachers might be remembering me and missing me and thinking what a fine pupil I'd been and how you wouldn't find another one like me in a hurry. I was sure that at least one of them must be thinking that. Because, like I said, I was always the first with his hand up in the air. Sometimes I'd even shout out the answer before the teacher had even finished asking the question. Not that they always appreciated this. In fact, a lot of the time my answer was completely wrong. Or it was the right answer, only it was the right answer to a different question, and not the one they'd asked.

"You're always jumping the gun, Harry!" they'd say, and, "Try not to be so impulsive."

And maybe if I wasn't, I'd still be alive today. But I am. And I'm not. And there you are.

I went across the playground—more flying than walking—over to where Mr. Diamond stood, trying to keep an eye on everyone and to maintain order and to nip any bullying in the bud.

"Mr. Diamond," I began, "it's Harry, come back on a visit and—"

But he plainly couldn't hear me and wasn't thinking of me, either, because as I spoke he glanced down at his wristwatch, rummaged in his coat pocket, took out his whistle, and gave it such a good hard blow that he went bright red in the face.

For a moment I was afraid he was going to have a heart attack.

But then I thought that if he did, I'd be able to help him. I got quite excited and almost started to look forward to it happening. Because if he dropped down dead, right there on the playground, I'd be able to give him a few hints and a few tips about being dead and stuff. I thought he'd probably appreciate that. Because it's nice to see some familiar faces when you're having a strange experience, and he'd probably enjoy the company. In fact, I could introduce him to Arthur, and we could take him up to the Desk and get him checked in and then show him round the Other Lands, give him a bit of a guided tour and point out the Great Blue Yonder.

Mr. Diamond blew his whistle again. He was more beetroot-colored than letter box–colored now. He definitely looked on the way out to me. He'd be keeling over clutching at his chest any second, I reckoned. Probably be dead within the minute. Might even whack his head on that paving slab just by him as he fell. That would definitely do for him, even if the heart attack didn't.

I mean, don't get me wrong, it wasn't that I wished him dead or anything, far from it. I was just so set on giving him a big welcome and on seeing the surprise and delight on his face when he realized it was me that I could hardly wait for it to happen.

He blew his whistle a third time. He was looking really bad now. His bald bits had gone red, too, it wasn't just his face.

"Come on, everyone!" he shouted. "End of break time! Let's get to our classes!"

He half raised his whistle back to his lips. One more

blow, that was all it needed, just one more little blow and he'd be with us.

But no. The children in the playground stopped playing, the games of catch and football fizzled out, the skipping ropes were rolled up and put away, the hopscotch stones were kicked aside, and everyone started to file back into school. Another blast wasn't needed.

Mr. Diamond lowered his whistle and put it away in his pocket. He'd been spared for another day. He probably didn't even realize what a narrow escape he'd had. But, then, no one ever does. Mostly you never do notice your narrow escapes—you only notice it when you've been caught.

The Peg

I turned and looked back at Arthur. He was still there, perched on top of the gatepost, quite happy, looking like he was in no hurry and had all the time in the world—which he did, in a way. I mean, it wasn't as if he had any urgent appointments, or as if he needed to get his homework done for the next morning.

"I'm just popping inside for a mo, Arthur!" I called to him, and I pointed toward the school. "That all right? You don't mind waiting? You all right up there?"

He made a face and gave a shrug, as if to say he didn't much care one way or the other and it was all the same to him. I thought that maybe he was getting a bit huffy at being left on his own, so I said, "Do you want to come in with me?"

But he shook his head. "No, thanks, Harry. I'm all right here. I'll wait."

"Won't be long, then," I called. And I turned and followed the others into school.

It hadn't changed much, the old place. But then you'd hardly have expected it to in a few weeks. There were some different posters and paintings up on the wall and some new bulletins on the bulletin board. I stopped to read them, but there was nothing there about me. I was sure there must have been, but it had probably been taken down.

It had probably been quite a big business at first around the school, me winding up dead. I daresay that they'd have had some prayers and some special mentions for me at morning assembly, with Mr. Hallent up at the front telling everybody what a credit to the school I'd been and what a terrible loss it was not to have me cluttering the place up anymore.

He had to say that, really, true or not. Because you can't go saying nasty things about people, not when they're dead, or at least not until they've been dead a fair old time—it's looked on as rude.

He'd probably have taken the opportunity to say a few words about road safety, too. And he'd have told everyone to be extra-special careful whenever they went out on their bikes.

To be fair, though, as I've said already, the accident wasn't my fault. And although I did maybe have a reputation as being a bit of a nutter for certain things, I was always careful on my bike. Because, after all, who wants to get flattened by a ten-ton truck? Certainly not me. But that's what happened. Which only goes to show that you never know what's coming round the corner.

So I thought of that assembly, and all the prayers and hymn singing and everyone saying what a nice bloke I'd been, and not a dry eye in the hall. I was sorry to have missed it, to tell the truth, because it would have been nice to have eavesdropped on that.

I was sorry I'd missed my funeral, too. I was more disappointed about that than anything. Because if there's one thing you really don't want to miss out on, it's your own funeral. I'd have loved to have seen all the kids from school there, and all my friends and all our relatives and all the neighbors and everyone, and Mum and Dad and Eggy. I know I'd have been upset, and it would have upset me even more to have seen Mum and Dad and Eggy crying for me, but I'd like to have been there, all the same—if only to have said goodbye.

Sometimes it does you good to cry, I reckon, and to feel sad. And if I'd been there, I could have said a proper goodbye to them, just like they were saying to me. I could have gone around the church and whispered a few words to everyone in person. I know they wouldn't have been able to hear me, but the thought would have been there.

"Goodbye, Uncle Charlie. Thanks for all the book vouchers," I could have said.

"Farewell, Auntie Peg. Thanks for all the hankies at Christmas. No one uses hankies now; it's all paper tissues. But they came in useful for making little parachutes for my plastic soldiers when I used to chuck them out the bedroom window, so thanks just the same."

I'd have said a proper goodbye to them all, especially to Mum and Dad and Eggy. I'd have put my ghostly arms around them and told them how much I loved them and how sorry I was to have left them, but they weren't to worry, as I wasn't suffering and wasn't unhappy and I was OK. I'd have apologized for all the trouble I'd caused them whenever I was having one of my difficult days. (I had a fair few of them, too.) And I'd have thanked them for having me. And I'd have said that just because my life was a short one, that didn't mean it hadn't been good, and I'd enjoyed it on the whole, and we'd had some good laughs and some good times, and I had no complaints.

No reproaches and no complaints and a big "Thank you" and a big "I love you" to them all. And a special word to Eggy, too, apologizing for what I'd said to her those few minutes before the truck got me. And she wasn't to feel bad, either, about what she'd said to me, because I knew she hadn't meant it, and it was just one of those things that people say in the heat of the moment.

Yes, I wished I could have been there. I wished could have been at the church for my funeral.

Mind you, I don't know if I'd have followed them on to the cemetery. I'm not so sure about that. It would have felt just a bit *too* odd, that would. I might have had trouble with that. It would have been bad enough seeing my coffin in the church there, with me inside. But to go along to the cemetery with it and to see what was left of me being stuck in a hole, and to see Mum and Dad and Eggy crying something terrible, that would have been more than I could bear. That would have broken my heart. I'd probably have started crying real tears myself, ghost or not. No, it was probably just as well that I'd missed it, really, best thing.

In fact, I did wonder if things weren't arranged so that you *couldn't* ever actually get to your own funeral. The way time passes on Earth and the way it passes once you've passed on are very different. Once you're dead, it seems that you've only spent a couple of hours standing in the queue at the check-in Desk, but in Earth time it must be days, or even weeks. And you're not supposed to go back, anyway. You're supposed to stay where you are or make your way to the Great Blue Yonder. It's only people like Arthur and me who've been a bit sort of nutterish in their lives and who've still got a spot of unfinished business—we're the only ones who even think of nipping back to see what's going on and to maybe do a bit of haunting.

So, on reflection, I wasn't so disappointed that I had missed the trip to the cemetery. But I did wish I'd been able to go to the church service and that I'd been there for the morning assembly at school when they'd all talked about me and said what a nice bloke I was. I'd have liked that bit. It would have been all right. And I maybe could have clapped at the end.

I went on into the school building, trooping along with the others, just like my name was still on the register. There I was, striding along with the rest, with them all nattering away around me, twenty-seven to the dozen. The only difference was that I was a sort of spirit now, invisible, inaudible, and probably inedible as well.

As we headed for the classroom, we passed the line of pegs for the coats, the one with the bench beneath it that you leave your lunch box on when you bring sandwiches instead of having school lunch.

Anyway, as we walked past the coat pegs, I stopped to have a look and see what had happened to mine. I wasn't entirely sure what to expect. They'd probably have put a brass plaque up there, that would have been the most likely thing. One of those little brass ones, like they have outside solicitor's offices, with names on them like *Bunkley, Snort and Wampsnurkle, Solicitors & Commissioners for Oaths.*

So that was what I imagined, a brass plate underneath my old peg. Or maybe one of those other types of plates, like the ones they have outside old houses where famous people used to live, stuck to the wall. Yeah, I thought, that would be a nice touch, to have a plate up there by my old peg. Only instead of saying something like *Albert Einstein lived here,* it would have said *Harry Decland hung his coat on this very peg. Harry was a famous pupil at this school.*

But when I looked, I couldn't find my peg there at all. I thought at first that my memory must have gone, or maybe my eyes were playing tricks on me. There had to be some kind of a mistake, surely. You couldn't have a peg one day and then not have it the next. Pegs didn't just disappear. So I looked closely, I peered everywhere, but it was nowhere to be seen. And yet I was *sure* it had been there, right there between Harriet Wilson's peg and Ben Jutley's. Right there, slap bang between them, right where this new name was, this "Bob Anderson" or whoever he was. I couldn't understand it, I simply could not understand where—

And then, of course, I did understand. But even then, even when the penny finally dropped and the cogs all clicked into place, I still couldn't believe it, I simply couldn't take it in.

They'd gone and given my peg to somebody else!

No plate, no brass plaque, no mention of the famous Harry and how tragic it all was, nothing of the sort. *They'd given my peg to Bob Anderson.*

Bob Anderson, eh? He had to be a new kid, because I'd not heard of him before. So maybe there was some excuse for him on those grounds. He probably hadn't known any better. That meant it was more likely all Mr. Hallent's fault. Yeah! Mr. Hallent, the headmaster, he'd be behind it. This Bob Anderson wouldn't have just gone and helped himself to my peg just like that. Someone in authority had told him to do it. Mr. Hallent, it had to be.

Well, of all the—the nerve. I felt betrayed. Betrayed and let down and bitterly disappointed. To give somebody else my peg to hang their coat on, and my spot on the bench to park their lunch box on, too. It didn't bear thinking about. It almost made me turn in my grave.

I'd spent so long standing there gawping at my old peg that it was several minutes before I realized that I was alone. The corridors had emptied, save for a few stragglers and latecomers, the doors had all closed, and the lessons were under way.

I gave my old peg one last look to make sure I hadn't made a mistake. But no. It was someone else's now. There was no doubt about it.

Mr. Hallent, the headmaster, came along the corridor then, in a tearing hurry, same as usual, probably off to stand in for a teacher who was ill.

"Mr. Hallent," I said. "Excuse me. I don't mean to complain, but was it you who changed my peg?"

But he didn't stop. He just looked right through me. And then he walked right through me as well.

I stood there seething a bit. I surprised myself at how upset I got. You'd never imagine that being dead could put you into such a horrible mood. Only, it wasn't being dead that had done it so much as feeling—well, dishonored. I thought they'd remember me always. But they seemed to have forgotten about me in five minutes flat.

When I'd calmed down, I went on along the corridor to find my old class and to take a peek inside. It would be different in there, I knew that. It would practically be a shrine. They'd have dedicated the whole room to my memory. They weren't like Mr. Hallent in there, not my old friends and classmates, nor my old teacher Mrs. Throggy (Mrs. Throgmorton in full). She was all right, really. Strict but fair. Good and kind and with a sense of humor (not like some *headmasters* I could mention.)

As I continued down the corridor, I peered into 4B to see how they were getting on. They all had their heads down and Mr. Collis was giving them a spelling test. Serve 'em right, I thought. I was sure they hadn't learned their words, either. And I bet they wouldn't have had any warning. It was one of his surprise tests, you could tell.

I went on. I glanced in on 5A, where everyone seemed to be doing geography. Then I prepared myself for what might await me. Because my old classroom was next in line, and I wasn't really sure what to expect.

Then it suddenly came to me—*black armbands!* That's what they'd be doing. They'd all be sitting in there wearing black armbands and talking in hushed whispers. That would definitely be it. That's what Mrs. Throggy would have them doing. Whenever they came back to class after break time, they'd have to put black armbands on and talk in hushed whispers, in honor of my memory. And maybe even wear dark glasses, too, so's you couldn't see how much they'd been crying. And big hankies as well, for blowing their noses on.

That would be it. I could hardly wait to see it.

I put on a spurt of speed and hurried down the corridor.

In Class

As I got to the classroom door, I slowed down and then stopped altogether. I made myself not look inside straightaway. I stood there, savoring the moment, sort of postponing the good bit, kind of saving the best for last, like you do with your dinner sometimes, when you get the carrots and the cabbage over with so that you can really enjoy the chips.

I decided that before I went inside I would hold a minute's silence in my memory. Not that I could really make a noise, even if I'd wanted to. But as a lot of the time silence is more inside you, anyway, that didn't seem to matter, because, like people say, it's the thought that counts.

So I stood there, looking down at my shoes, and I slowly counted up to sixty, giving each second its full value and not rushing any of them, but pacing them properly, going, "A thousand and one, a thousand and two, a thousand and three . . ." just like you're supposed to.

As I bowed my head and had my minute silence, people passed me in the corridor. I saw big feet and little feet, men's shoes and women's shoes and girl's shoes and boy's shoes go by. But I didn't look up to see who they belonged to. I just went on with paying myself my last respects. Because you should, really. You should at least be a bit sorry that you're dead. If you're not, who will be?

They must have held quite a few of those minute silences since I'd been gone, I thought. They'd probably had one at morning assembly, all standing there with bowed heads and trying not to fidget or to get the giggles—like you do even when it's serious, or in some ways just because it *is* so serious, though I don't know why.

I could see them all, the whole school, all the pupils, all the teachers, Mr. Hallent up on the podium, his head bowed so that you could see where he was losing his hair.

I felt sorry for them all, and a bit sad, and I felt a bit distinguished, too, and that it was all pretty special that I should be the cause of all this silence and glumness. Because I was just a bit of a mucker-about, really, in some ways, and it's funny that even someone who did a lot of mucking about is still highly thought of when he's dead.

"A thousand and thirty-five, a thousand and thirty-six . . ."

I was tempted to look up and peer inside, but no, I stuck to my guns and forced myself to keep staring at the floor.

". . . a thousand and thirty-seven, a thousand and thirty-eight . . ."

What would it be like in there? What would I see? It

wasn't that hard to imagine. I could see my old desk in there, all sort of strewn with flowers and kind of turned into a little sort of holy shrine. Maybe Martina—who was good at art and stuff—would have done one of her paper cutouts, like she did, with all the fancy bits on it. And then Graham Best would have written something on a paper scroll in his best italic handwriting—which was so good it was just like it had been printed out on the computer.

Harry's Desk, it would read. *In loving memory of our dear departed classmate, Harry. Gone, but never forgotten. He will live forever in our hearts and our homework. The football team will never be the same without him, and will, in fact, be dead lucky if it ever wins another game.*

I crossed the "dead" out then, in my mind's eye, as it didn't seem quite respectful enough. Just "very lucky" would have to do instead. I also made a mental note to nip down to the noticeboard in the assembly hall later and have a quick look at the football results to see how the team had been getting on without me. They'd have been having a bad season, obviously. Probably even have been losing by scores like 10–0, or 20–0, or even 55–0. I felt a bit bad about it, about dying and leaving them without a decent midfielder, but there you are. That's football, I suppose.

"A thousand and fifty-five, a thousand and fifty-six . . ."

I suddenly thought about Arthur, waiting for me out there on top of the gatepost. If he *was* still waiting, of course. He might have got fed up and hopped it. I had a moment of panic then, wondering how on earth I'd ever get back to the Other Lands without him. But then I thought, No, he wouldn't go without me.

"A thousand and fifty-eight, a thousand and fifty-nine . . ."

I could see it all so clearly now, and it seemed so sad I almost wanted to cry again. I could see my desk there in the classroom, with a little vase of flowers on it, or maybe just a single red rose. And there would be a fresh single red rose every day. The withered one would be gone and a new one with velvet-like petals would be in its place every morning, and nobody would really know how it got there. But it would be Olivia who had done it. Olivia Masterson, who had always liked me and who had told her friend Tilly that she had been in love with me once. Only Tilly hadn't kept it to herself and had told Petra, who had gone and told everyone. And then all the boys found out, and they all used to tease her at break time—at least, for a while, until they got fed up with it and found something else to go on about.

"Olivia's in love with Harry, Olivia's in love with Harry!"

Most of the time she just ignored them—which is the best thing to do when people are being stupid like that. But even ignoring people can get difficult, and Mrs. Throggy had to tell them all to pack it in and to stop acting so daft, which they did eventually.

As far as I was concerned, I just acted dead cool about it. And when Pete came up and said, "Olivia says she's in love with you, Harry," I just acted all nonchalant about it, like it was all the same to me, and like that sort of thing was always happening and that people were always falling in love with me all the time, on account of my good looks and winning ways and natural charm and magnetic personality.

But they weren't. Not really. No one had ever been in love with me before.

But I never said anything, mind, not to Olivia. I just ignored her and tried to avoid her as much as possible, and I definitely made sure that we were *never* left on our own together. Because, you see, if we'd ever been spotted on our own, then it might have given rise to rumors that I was in love with her, too. Which, of course, I wasn't, as that was for wimps. And while it wasn't so bad for people to go round saying, "Olivia loves Harry," for them to have gone round saying, "Harry loves Olivia" would have been the pits.

Sometimes, though, maybe during a lesson, I might sneak a look at her—when no one could see me sneaking it—and to be honest, she was ever so nice and really pretty, and I didn't mind that she was in love with me, at all. In fact, I rather liked it in some ways, because it made me feel that I was special and it made me feel all warm inside.

And the funny thing, you know, was that after a while I did begin to love her a little bit, too. Just because she was in love with me. Isn't that strange? I'd never really thought of her much before, but now that I'd found out that she was in love with me, I sort of saw her in a different light and could see that she was nice, really, and that she had a lot of good qualities, and I thought about her a lot of the time.

I even got a Valentine as well, back on Valentine's Day, February 14th. I'm not saying she sent it, because it wasn't signed. All it said was "From an admirer." It might have been from her, or it might have been from someone else, doing it as a joke, to make me think that it was from her when it wasn't. But the other thing is that she got a Valentine, too, or so I heard. And it was also unsigned and it also had "From an admirer" on it. And when she brought it into class and showed it to her friends, some of them said that it looked like my writing—though I didn't see how they could have said that, because I reckoned that whoever had written it would have used their left hand—if they were right-handed. Or their right hand if they were left-handed, so as to disguise their writing. But the *other* hand, anyway, not their proper, usual hand, if you see what I mean.

So that was what I said, anyway, and I don't know why anyone could have reckoned that I'd sent it at all.

"A thousand and sixty!"

My minute's silence was up. It was time to look in. Time to enter my old classroom. Time to see my desk, now a shrine, with a little candle burning on it, and with the decorations and the scroll, and the single dark red rose, with the small drop of water upon it, which looked at first like a dewdrop but which was really a lonely tear, probably belonging to Olivia Masterson.

I walked through the door. (No, that's not a mistake, I didn't open it first, I just walked right through it.) Mrs. Throggy was teaching math.

"And so if we divide by a hundred, where should the decimal point go?"

My hand went up immediately, and before I could stop myself I was going, "Miss! Miss! Me, Miss!"

She pointed straight at me.

"Yes, over there, you"—only instead of adding

"Harry," she said, "Olivia," and she looked right through me.

Stupid, really. For a moment there I'd thought I was still alive.

I turned to see what Olivia was going to say, and to see how she'd been taking my sad demise—pretty badly, probably. She'd be distraught, no doubt about it.

"The decimal point goes after the second five, Miss."

"That's it, Olivia, well done."

But no. Olivia didn't look distraught in the least. But that wasn't all. It wasn't just that there were no black arm-bands, that no one was wearing dark glasses, or talking in hushed whispers, or blowing their nose into a tearful hanky.

It was my desk. My *desk!* My *precious* desk! My desk that should have been like a shrine, like a tombstone, like a permanent memorial to my memory. My desk! The terrible truth was . . .

Someone else was sitting at it!

Yes, I know. Incredible! But it was true. There were no flowers, no candles, no scrolls, no nothing. There was a new boy sitting at my desk!

"OK," Mrs. Throggy was saying, "we'll go on to something else now, and do a little more work on negative numbers."

That came as a shock, too. Negative numbers. What did I know about negative numbers? Not a lot. Not a lot about negative numbers or negative anythings. The only negatives I knew much about were the ones you got back from the drugstore when you took your holiday snaps in to be developed. Something else had moved on without me. My old schoolmates were learning new lessons; they knew things that I didn't.

They turned their books to the right pages. I studied the boy who was sitting at my desk, to see if he had anything lying there that might give a clue to his identity. There was nothing I could see on his math book, but then as he picked his ruler up to draw a straight line, I made out a name on it, scratched into the plastic.

Bob, it read. *Bob Anderson.*

So!

So this was *him!* This was the sleazy, slimy Bob Anderson. This was the rat who had gone and stepped into a dead boy's shoes. This was the one who had nabbed my peg for his coat and collared my space on the bench for his lunch box. Me, barely laid to rest in the cemetery, and here he was, pinching all my stuff like it belonged to him, and always had done, just like I'd left it all to him in my will. But I hadn't. I hadn't even made a will. And even if I had, why would I leave all my belongings to someone I didn't know?

So! Bob Anderson! This was *him*. Why, I'd half a mind to give him a good thumping. (Well, half a mind to give him a good haunting, anyway.)

First my peg, then my lunch box space, and now my desk. And what next? What else of mine had he got? Why, he was probably even wearing my shirt number in the football team.

And then I saw Olivia look across and smile at him, and I thought that he was probably going to get my Valentine cards as well. He really had, he'd gone and pinched everything—my peg, my lunch box space, my desk, probably my place in the football team, and to top it all, my Valentines.

It just didn't seem fair. This Bob Anderson wasn't as big as me, or as good-looking, and he certainly hadn't put his hand in the air and shouted, "Me, Miss, me! I know!" when Mrs. Throggy had asked a question. So he probably wasn't as intelligent as me, either.

He just happened to be alive, that was all. And it didn't seem right. People who haven't got half your good looks and abilities, they pinch your peg and they steal your desk and your fond admirers, and why?—just because they're alive. That's why. Just because he was alive and I wasn't. What a creep. I absolutely hated him. I didn't know where he had come from, but I hated him for taking my place.

"OK," Mrs. Throggy was saying, "now to recap. What do you get when you multiply two negative numbers together? Peter?"

"A positive number, Miss."

"Good. And what do you get when you multiply three negative numbers together?"

She seemed to look toward me. But it was no use in asking me. I didn't know. I'd missed out on all that, I'd slipped behind. What did I know about multiplying three negative numbers together? No use asking me, I was dead.

I stood there a while, invisible in the classroom. I looked around at all my old friends and classmates. I looked at this new boy who had come to take my place. I turned and looked at Mrs. Throggy, and listened to her voice. Was there a catch in it? A note of sorrow? A note of sadness for her long-lost pupil Harry? There didn't seem to be. Not at all. "Life goes on," people say. "Nobody's indispensable." And it seemed to be true. Because here was life, going on as if I had never existed, and it seemed that I was as dispensable as an old empty drink carton, used up, finished with, thrown away, and worst of all— forgotten.

I looked at Bob Anderson. He was chewing the end of his pencil and looking like he was having trouble understanding his negative numbers.

"When you multiply two negative signs together, once cancels the other out, and so you end up with a positive," Mrs. Throggy was saying.

But it was all Chinese to Bob Anderson and me. It was probably all Chinese to even Chinese people.

I felt a wave of sympathy for him, and I suddenly didn't hate him so much anymore. After all, it wasn't this Bob Anderson's fault that he had taken my place. He'd probably just come along, maybe moved into the area with his mum and dad, and they'd looked for a place for him at the nearest school. And they'd found mine. He was quite innocent, really. He probably hadn't even known that it was my peg and that it still would be if it hadn't been for the truck.

It was the rest of them. They were to blame. It was *their* fault for letting him take it all over. It was *their* fault for not telling him, not stopping him, for not explaining to him that my desk and peg and lunch box space were like holy articles and sort of tombstones to my memory.

How could they have let it happen? All the people I had thought were my friends. How could they have forgotten me so soon? Pete and Olivia and Mrs. Throggy and Mr. Hallent and everyone on the football team. There was nothing in the classroom to remember me, nothing at all. Not one single, solitary black armband on anyone's sleeve.

"Now, if you add a positive number to a negative number that is greater than the positive number . . ."

And then I saw it. I turned and there it was, up on the wall behind me. It covered every inch. There were poems and pictures and drawings and paintings and memories and mementos and photos that people had brought in. And along the top of the wall, in big cutout letters were the words *Our Friend Harry*.

And that was me. It was all about me. The whole wall, the whole great big wall, every inch of it, all covered with—well, it embarrasses me to tell you, really, after the horrible things I said about everyone forgetting me. But everyone was so nice. It was unbelievable, really, all the things people wrote and said. Even the people who hadn't liked me, just as much as the ones that had.

There was a poem up there, on a white piece of paper stuck on to a blue card and decorated with dried, pressed flowers, and it was called *Just Harry* and it was signed *Olivia*. And I don't really want to tell you what it said, as it's a bit sort of personal and private—even if it was stuck up on the wall for everyone to see. But if I'm honest with you, I felt a bit upset after I read it, just like you feel when you're going to cry. Not that I ever did cry, not much, as anyone could tell you, 'cause I was well known for being pretty tough and all.

Then there was a sort of essay up there, too, entitled *My Mate Harry* and this was written by Pete. But it wasn't sort of sad stuff, it was really funny, more like a sort of celebration. And Pete had written down all the things that we'd got up to, even the stuff about us getting into trouble. But it didn't *seem* like trouble, the way he'd written it, it all sounded like it was lots of fun and a real good laugh—more fun than I'd remembered. And it was so good, I had to read through it a couple of times, just to remind myself that it was really me he was talking about. And he said a bit about the both of us in the football team, and about that time we went off in the bus for the away game and how when we got there I discovered I'd lost my shorts. And he remembered how the only spare pair we could find was the red pair, and so I had to play the game in this red pair of shorts, and how everyone called me the red devil for a while after. And although it wasn't *that* funny at the time, the way Pete put it, it seemed really great and like we'd had a tremendous time together, and that I'd sort of had a marvelous life.

And maybe I had. Maybe I *had* had a marvelous life. The way Pete wrote it, it made me think I had. And, you know, at the bottom or Pete's essay, Mrs. Throggy had written, "Thank you, Peter, for this wonderful depiction of Harry and of Harry's life. We will all miss him more than we can ever say, but thank you for putting our feelings into these words and for reminding us what a unique and wonderful character he was. He was so life-enhancing and full of curiosity and fun and no one will ever be able to take his place in our hearts. I'm sure that Harry would be pleased to know that he was so loved and valued by us all."

But I didn't. I didn't feel pleased. I just felt like crying again. I just felt like crying because I'd had such good friends and I'd gone and thought they'd forgotten me. But they hadn't. And I felt ashamed.

"Now, if we subtract minus six from minus four, what will . . ."

Mrs. Throggy's voice droned on like background music—well, like a background voice, anyway. I read everything that was up there on the wall in "Harry's Corner," and I looked at all the drawings and the photos and took in everyone's memories of me.

You'd think I'd been the best thing since sliced bread, according to everything up there, the best invention since computers, that was me. In fact, you'd have had a hard job working out quite how the world was managing without me—though it seemed to be getting by all the same.

Even as I read all the tributes and accolades, there was one I was especially looking for. I maybe didn't admit it to myself, but there was one contribution I particularly wanted to see. And then I finally found it, down at the bottom right-hand corner of the wall, partially hidden by an enlarged photo of me and the rest of the class, taken about eight months ago. There it was. The one thing I did, and yet didn't, want to read. It wasn't a very long essay, but it easily filled three pages, being done in a big, scrawling hand.

Harry, it was titled. That was all. Not "Memories of Harry" or "Dearly Beloved Harry." Just "Harry." Yes. *Harry*, it read, by *J. Donkins*.

The J stood for John, even if—as far as most of us were concerned—it more usually stood for Jelly. And that's what it was, the final tribute of my sworn enemy. What could *he* possibly find to say that was nice about me? Because I certainly couldn't think of anything nice to say about him.

Harry, by J. Donkins.

He'd probably have felt he had to say something nice about me just because I was dead. I hate that, though, when people go all gooey on you, just because you're dead. I mean, a friend's a friend and a foe's a foe. You shouldn't really go saying nice things about people just because they're dead. Not if you don't mean them. It's better not to say anything at all.

Harry, by J. Donkins.

There he was, sitting at his desk, trying to come to terms with negative numbers, and not finding it too easy. What would he say if he knew I was standing there, able to read what he'd written?

What, indeed?

I took a deep breath—at least, in my mind I did—and I read on.

Jelly

"Me and Harry was never big mates . . ." the essay began, and I thought to myself, No, well, you can say that again.

He didn't have very good writing, did Jelly. It was big and clumsy, just like him. And where he had written "was," as in "Me and Harry *was* never big mates," Mrs. Throggy had crossed out "was" and had lightly written "were" next to it in pencil. She had obviously given up on correcting it after that, though. Maybe she didn't feel it was right, seeing it was supposed to be my obituary and it wasn't really something to be marked. So she let the rest of it stand, just as Jelly had written it, with blots and smudges and all.

Harry, by J. Donkins
Me and Harry was never big mates, not really, though, to be honest, I don't really know why. We just seemed to get off on the

wrong foot somehow, from right back in the
infants' class, when we were small. I don't
know if maybe I'd done something to offend
Harry that I never knew about, or if maybe
he just didn't like the look of me much or
something, but the truth is we never really
hit it off and he even got me once round at
the back of the gym.

I tried to be mates with Harry lots of
times, and I was always asking him if he
fancied a kick-about. But he would never play
with my football—almost like there was germs
on it or something, or like there was
something wrong with me.

It was Harry who started called me Jelly,
'cause I'm a bit fat, and maybe once he'd
started doing that, I wasn't so nice to him,
either, because thanks to him everyone else
called me Jelly, too. So I maybe started calling
him names and stuff so as to maybe try and
get my own back. And it was me who stole his
football shorts that time we went to the away
match on the bus, when he had to wear the red
ones. But even then he still sort of came out of
it all right, because everyone called him the red
devil and I think he liked that, really. But I'm
sorry for nicking his shorts. I shouldn't have
done that, and I'll send his mum the money so
as to get some flowers for him and to try and
make it up, and that's a promise.

But it wasn't me who started the nastiness between us, at least I don't think so, and I was only ever nasty to him because he'd hurt my feelings. I suppose I wanted him to feel hurt, too, like I felt. So it's true that I wasn't very nice to Harry, and I'm sorry, and I didn't really mean it. But he wasn't very nice to me, either, and that's true as well.

I used to wish Harry would be my mate sometimes, and I wished there was something I could do to change things. But it just seemed like we would be enemies forever and that was it. I did like Harry in a lot of ways, though, even though I'd never have admitted it. 'Cause he was very funny sometimes and it would be hard not to laugh at his jokes. But I'd sit there all the same, biting my lip and scowling and trying not to laugh, 'cause I didn't want him thinking that he was funny, even though he was.

I'm sorry that Harry's dead, because it means I can never make it right now. I can never be mates with him or say I'm sorry for the times I was nasty. And I can never forgive him, either, for the times he was nasty to me. Maybe he wouldn't want me to forgive him, maybe he wouldn't want to be my friend, anyway, not ever. I don't know. But just because someone's not your friend, that doesn't mean you aren't sorry when they're gone. I did like Harry, really, he was very funny at times, and good at football, and he understood things a lot quicker than I did, and he was quite clever and he made me feel like dozy lump, though I'd never had told him that.

If Harry could come back now, I'd go up to him and put my hand out and ask him if we couldn't let bygones be bygones and try and leave each other alone in the future, even if we could never be friends.

So I'm sorry that Harry's gone, I am, really, and that's true, I'm not just saying that. And funnily enough, I think that if it had been the other way round and I'd had the accident, Harry would have been sorry in the same way, too. And the worst part of it is that I can never make it right now. That's the bit that's hardest of all. So, I'm sorry, Harry, but I just want you to know that it was my idea about the tree. The tree was my idea. And that's my way of trying to make things up. Bye, Harry. All the best.

And then it was signed *J. Donkins* at the bottom. What do you say? Where do you go to? How do you begin? I had to sit down. Not that I really could, of course, but I had that have-to-sit-down feeling. So I went and sat on the edge of Mrs. Throggy's desk and tried to take it all in and to make sense of it.

Me? Not like Jelly? It was the other way round, surely, right from way back. *He'd* started it, hadn't he, calling me beanpole and stuff, and so I'd retaliated by calling him Jelly. But I'd *never* picked on him, not *once*, ever. It has *him* who'd picked on *me*. And it *wasn't* true that I wouldn't play football with him—I would have done loads of times, only *he* always went on about how it was *his* ball. And as soon as he started losing or if he ever got a kick on the shin, he'd go and pick *his* ball up and say, "That's it, I'm not playing now." And we'd say, "Come on, Jelly, be a sport, at least let's finish the game." But he wouldn't let us because it was *his* ball, and if he couldn't play with it, then nobody could.

So it wasn't my fault. It never had been. It wasn't my fault, at all—was it? And yet all the same, you couldn't help but wonder. It made you think, right enough, it did.

I went back over to my memorial wall and I reread his essay about me all the way through. Then I went and stood behind Jelly himself, as he sat there at this desk, trying to come to terms with negative numbers. I looked at the splodgy ballpoint that he held between his podgy fingers. Was it true that he'd sort of liked me, really, and had almost laughed at my jokes? Or had he just said that because I was dead now and because you're supposed to say nice things when people die? Then I thought of the last bit he wrote, about how the worst thing of all was that he could never make it right now, he could never patch it up with me because I wasn't there to patch it up with. And I could understand that, because that was how

I felt about my sister, Eggy, that I could never patch it up with her. And I felt that Jelly and I both knew what it was to have unfinished business.

I put out my hand. "Friends, then, Jelly?" I said. "Shake on it?"

He went on with his work. He was getting the sum that Mrs. Throggy had given them all wrong. Even I could see that. And what I knew about negative numbers could be written on the back of a very small stamp.

"Friends, Jelly, OK? No hard feelings? All right?"

But he just stubbornly went on with his calculations, smudging blobs of greasy ink all over himself and his bit of paper, mucking it all up and getting it all podgy and wrong, just like he always did. In fact, that was what used to annoy you so much about him—him getting it so podgy wrong and being so clumsy all the time.

"Friends, then, Jelly? OK?"

If only I could make him hear me. If only there was some way I could make a noise, even if only inside his head, where he alone would hear it, like some kind of telepathy or thought transference, like bending spoons and stuff.

"Jelly, it's Harry. I'm sorry about us not getting on. No bad feelings now, eh?"

I thought it at him as hard as I could. I watched his face for some flicker of understanding, but no, nothing. He just went on getting his sums wrong, his chubby cheeks set in place like two big jellies in a mold.

"*Jelly!*" I tried to shout into his head. "*Jelly!* It's *me, Harry!* I'm here right next to you and I've just read your essay in the memorial corner. I haven't come back to haunt you, Jelly, or to go *Boo!* in your ear and give you nightmares or to get you started back on the bed-wetting again. I just wanted to say I'm sorry, too, Jel, that we didn't get on while I was still alive. I thought you didn't like me, Jel, and it seems you thought I didn't like you. I think we just had a bit of a misunderstanding, Jel, that's all. Do you understand? Just a misunderstanding. So don't feel bad about anything, and I won't, either. That's us evens now, Jelly, OK? Even-steven. All right? OK, Jelly, OK?"

But no. Nothing. I may as well have been trying to communicate with a big hamburger, sitting there in its bun. And as I looked at Jelly, I thought that was just what he looked like, like a great big undercooked hamburger with a piece of tomato on top for a head, with a bun for clothes, and with two chips sticking out where his legs should be.

And I began to get annoyed with him all over again, just like when I was alive.

"Jelly! You great nit!" I thought at him. "Can't you pay attention when I'm forgiving you here and trying to make things square all round! What's up, haven't you got any brains or something!"

But he just went on, getting deeper and deeper into trouble with his math. He'd be lucky to get zero out of ten the way he was going on. In fact, Mrs. Throggy would probably give him a negative number for his negative numbers, like minus six out of ten. Mind you, knowing Jelly, he'd probably be proud of that and think it was rather good.

I was just about to give up on Jelly when I remembered Arthur and the fruit machine again and how he'd got the line of strawberries to come up. And I thought about the leaf I'd shaken from the tree. So, obviously, it was *possible* to alter things if you concentrated on them hard enough. I directed all my thoughts toward Jelly's ballpoint and tried to influence its movement.

"Minus six minus minus six equals sixty-six . . ." he was writing.

"Hello, Jelly, it's Harry here," I willed the pen to write. "It's Harry, it's *Harry,* it's—"

And then, without warning, Jelly's ballpoint suddenly flew out of his hand, shot halfway across the classroom, and landed with a clatter on Bob Anderson's desk (*my* desk, as was).

"'Ere!" he shouted. "What're you playing at, Jelly! Stop mucking about!" And he picked the pen up and went to throw it back, only Mrs. Throggy stopped him.

"I'll take that, thank you."

She took it over to Jelly.

"Whatever are you doing, John?"

"Sorry, Miss," Jelly Donkins said, "I was concentrating and it must have just sort of jumped out of my hand. Maybe I was pressing it down too hard or something. Sorry."

"Never mind, Just be more careful next time, that's all," and she gave Jelly back his pen. "Just try and be more careful."

Times I'd heard that—"Be more careful next time." When I think of all the narrow escapes and close shaves I'd had in my life, all the times I nearly came a cropper, all the times I nearly fell off things or almost did myself a serious injury.

"You were lucky then, Harry. Be more careful next time!"

Trouble is, it's never the same the next time, no matter how careful you are. It's always a different accident in a different way. And while you're being careful not to have the old accident again, you just go and have a new one instead. That's what happened to me. Once, about a year ago, I'd got the lace from one of my shoes caught in the chain of my bike. It had got wrapped all around it and the whole mess had seized up. So the bike had stopped, and *wallop!*—there I was, lying all over the pavement, covered in dents and bruises.

"You were lucky it wasn't much worse, Harry," my dad said. "You could have been killed. Always make sure that your laces are done up properly before you get on to your bike. Don't let it happen again."

So I hadn't. I'd always done my laces up really carefully after that, and if they were still long, I'd tuck them down into the sides of my shoes, especially so's they wouldn't get snagged round the chain or the spokes.

And so there I was, cycling along, when suddenly it feels as if my right shoelace has worked loose. Well, I don't want to have *another* accident, do I? Not in view of my past experience. So I just glance down for a moment, just to check that the lace is all right. I take my eyes off the road only for a fraction of a second, no more than that, but it's enough for me to lose control a little, and I start to veer out into the middle of the road, and I'm maybe wobbling a bit. And the next thing, this huge truck comes round the corner, way out in the middle of the road, too. Not that it should ever have been there, as it's a residential street and big trucks aren't supposed to come down that way. And the next thing I know—

And there you are. So much for being more careful next time.

Jelly sat there looking at his pen as if it had gone a bit mad.

"It just jumped out of my hand," he kept muttering. "Just jumped out of my hand. I was sitting here holding it, and it jumped right out of my hand."

"Come along now, John," Mrs. Throggy said. "Do try and finish the exercise."

I tried a few more times to move Jelly's pen and make it write out what I wanted it to. But I couldn't. It just didn't work. Maybe making the pen jump out of his hand had just been a fluke, a one-off. Maybe my mental energies were exhausted. Maybe it had had nothing to do with me, anyway, and Jelly had done it himself through pressing down on it too hard, like he'd said.

Either way, I couldn't seem to communicate with him to tell him that I'd read his essay about me and that I hoped we could be friends now and that there'd be no bad feelings on either side.

As it seemed I couldn't change anything, and as I'd seen all that I had come to see, then maybe it was time for me to go.

"Goodbye, everyone," I said. "Bye, Pete, bye, Olivia, bye, Mrs. Throggy, and everyone else. Bye, Bob Anderson, whoever you are. I hope you look after my desk and my peg and the space for my lunch box. I certainly shan't be needing lunch anymore. So bye, everyone. Thanks for everything. It was good to see you again, and thanks for all the nice things you wrote about me. Bye now. I'll always remember you. I'm sorry I won't be growing up with you all and going up to the next class and then to the bigger school. But good luck, anyway. Maybe I'll see you all again some day. Who knows. Bye, everyone, bye."

And then I left.

I didn't look back, as I think it's best not to look back too much or too often. Looking back can upset you. It doesn't do to dwell too much on what was and what might have been and what never will be now. So I pressed on down along the corridor, heading out for the playground and Arthur.

I paused on the way to look at the football line-up and to see who was playing in my old position on the team, and just as I'd suspected, it was Bob Anderson. There he was, in my old midfield spot. He seemed to be quite taking me over. And the team had won their last three matches as well. So they were getting on all right without me. Yes, a lot of things were getting on all right without me, and I remembered then what Arthur had said when I told him I wanted to pay a visit to my old school.

"Don't expect too much, Harry. Don't expect too much of people, and then you won't be disappointed."

And maybe I had expected too much. Though in some ways, maybe I had expected too little, too.

As I walked out of the school, I remembered something that Jelly Donkins had written in his essay about me, one of the last things he had said, something about a tree, and how it had all been his idea.

They must have planted a tree for me, then. I wondered where it would be. I walked around the back of the school, looking for signs of new trees and earth having been dug up recently. I found it over by the nature corner. I must have walked straight past it earlier, when I was looking for my worms. It was a sapling, surrounded by a sort of protective fence to keep the squirrels and the mice and the little kids off it.

There was a little engraved metal plate there, stuck into the ground next to it.

For Harry. From everyone in his class. With love.

And it gave my dates and how long I'd been in the school.

I stood there, contemplating my tree. Then I remembered Arthur and thought that he must be getting really fed up by now and that it was rude to keep him waiting and that I'd better get a move on.

"I see they did you a tree, Harry."

I turned and there he was, standing right next to me, looking at my tree.

"Do you know what it is?" I asked him, because I was never big on trees. Racing cars I know a bit, about but trees, no, not really.

"It's an oak, isn't it?" he said.

"Is it? I dunno. It's difficult to tell when they're little."

"I think so."

"They live a long time, don't they, oaks?"

"Hundreds of years," Arthur said. "Can do."

"Hundreds of years, eh?"

That made me feel quite good. I thought of my tree, growing and growing. I thought of all those hundreds of years going by. I thought of all the people who would come and go and who would shelter under my tree— from the rain in the autumn and from the sun in the summer. I thought of all the people who would read the little engraved plate stuck in the earth next to its roots. I thought of them thinking of me, wondering who old long-ago Harry was, and telling each other the story of me and my bike and the truck and how my friends had all had taken up a collection to buy me a tree. And maybe they'd remember, too, that it was all Jelly Donkin's idea. And maybe it would make them feel warm inside, and think that it wasn't such a bad world, after all.

Maybe.

I turned to Arthur. "It's a good tree, isn't it?" I said.

"Very nice," he nodded. "Very nice, indeed."

Then a thought came into my mind.

"Did anyone ever plant a tree for *you*, Arthur?" I asked.

He looked a bit uncomfortable and adjusted his hat on top of his head and scratched it a bit (his head, not his hat), which was a sort of nervous habit he'd got.

"Eh, yes," he said. "'Course they did. Quite a few, to be honest. More of a small wood, really, than a tree. Something of a forest, in fact. Quite a big one. The 'Good Old Arthur Memorial Forest' it was called. Only it got chopped down—for firewood. Otherwise, I'd take you round to see it."

"Ah," I said, "that was a pity."

I wondered if he was exaggerating. But then I thought that maybe he felt a bit jealous of my tree and was only trying to keep his end up so as not to appear totally tree-less, as though no one had ever cared for him. So I didn't press him on whereabout this forest of his had been and just went along with what he'd said.

I looked away and studied my tree again. I wondered how long it would last. Maybe it would get chopped down for firewood, too. Or a bulldozer would get it for a road-widening scheme. Or maybe it would die of Dutch elm disease. Or Dutch oak disease. Or measles—tree measles, that is. Or maybe a flying saucer would land on it or—

It didn't bear thinking about, all the things that could happen to my tree. I put them out of my mind. Why imagine the worst? I thought. The worst that can happen is that you'll die, and I had. So I might as well look on the bright side now. And maybe my tree would last for hundreds of years, and maybe it wouldn't. I could only hope that it would do its best. That's all you can hope of anyone or anything, that they'll do their best. Because trees are only sort of human, after all, in their way.

The Cinema

"Where to now?" I said to Arthur as we crossed the yard and walked away from the school. "What'll we do? More haunting?"

Arthur shrugged. "If you like," he said. "I don't care." And he took the ghost of an old-fashioned watch out of the ghost of his old-fashioned waistcoat pocket, and he gave it the ghost of a look, and then he put it away again.

"Shouldn't stay out too long," he said. "Ought to get back—you know."

"Yes," I agreed. "Ought to get back for—"

And do you know, what I nearly said was "Ought to get back for tea." Not that I was hungry. Not that it was even teatime. Not that even if I had been hungry and even if it had been teatime it would have made any difference, I still wouldn't have got any. There was no tea to be had up in the Other Lands. Nor down here, really. You could watch other people have their tea, I suppose, and sort of have it along with them, but it wouldn't be the same. More like watching a film of people eating than actually doing it for yourself.

Arthur seemed a bit faraway, like his mind wasn't on haunting or on tea, either. I suppose that when he'd been alive they'd have had meat pies for tea and a pint of beer for breakfast. I was sure I'd read that somewhere, or done it in history. But I guessed that Arthur was thinking about his mum again, and he probably didn't like to stay away from the Other Lands for too long in case she turned up and he missed her. I could just picture them meeting each other. There she'd be, with that ghost of a button missing off her blouse, and there he'd be, with that selfsame ghost of a button in his ghost of a hand. And they'd meet and match and be reunited at last, and all the unfinished business of theirs would be settled, and off they could go to the Great Blue Yonder, to whatever was there, and be at peace, and they'd not have to restlessly wander forever like—

Like ghosts.

"I suppose we could maybe do a *bit* more haunting," I said casually, not wanting to sound *too* keen. "Just to keep our hands in. Is there anything else we can do apart from tinkering with one-armed bandits?"

Arthur thought a moment. "Apart from jackpotting?"

"Nothing *too* wicked, mind," I said. "I wouldn't want to really upset anyone."

"No," Arthur said, "I wasn't thinking of anything like that—come on. There's somewhere I want to go."

"Hang on, Arthur!" I said. "Just a second! I wanted to ask—"

But he was already away. And I had no choice but to go after him.

We had left my old school behind us by now and were walking along into town, going in the direction of the plaza and the pedestrianized shopping center.

As we went along, I watched the people who passed us, looking for familiar faces and for those I once knew.

We shuffled along, Arthur and me, and had you been able to see us, you'd have thought we looked like anyone, just like any two boys on our way into town, maybe off to the Games Workshop to have a look at the latest War Hammers, or off to see what new computer games had come into the shops.

You might have wondered what we were doing out of school at that time of day and probably would have concluded that we were ditching. Or maybe, from the look of Arthur and from the clothes he was wearing, you might have thought he was on his way to audition for the part of the Artful Dodger in a forthcoming TV series, and that I was going along to keep him company and to see that he didn't get too nervous.

Yes, we looked as normal as anyone, really. Only, nobody *could* see us, that was the thing, even though we could see them, clear as mud. And it was odd to walk along, with your feet not really touching the ground at all, just floating by like a low-flying cloud, half an inch above the pavement. And if you sometimes forgot to look where you were going, you'd find that somebody had gone and walked straight through you, or even ridden right through you on a bicycle, and you hadn't even noticed—it hadn't hurt at all.

It was odd, too, to see how everyone has two faces—a public one and a private one. One for when they think other people are able to see them, the other for when they think they're alone. And sometimes people make an effort to look happy and they say, "Good morning, how are you, lovely day!" in a loud, cheerful voice, like they didn't have a care in the world. But when they think they're alone again, their smiles droop and their faces fall and they look miserable beyond belief.

Other times—which is even more curious—people make an effort to look *miserable*. Yes, I know, it's hard to believe, but they do. They meet someone in the street who says, "How are you? Are you well?" and they say, "No, I'm terrible, awful, you wouldn't believe how bad it is, I hardly know where to begin." But as soon as they part company, the person instantly cheers up and looks perfectly fine. In fact, it's almost as if telling other people that they're miserable is what makes them happy.

Anyway, on we went, Arthur and me, and he seemed to be heading for the shopping center.

I saw a friend of my mum's on the way; she had her youngest in a stroller. Its handles were weighed down with carrier bags.

"Hello, Mrs. Fraser!" I called. "How are you? It's me, Harry."

But she went on her way without a second glance. I didn't know why I'd done it, really. I knew she couldn't hear me.

We floated on into the town.

We were in the plaza now and just walking along by Dixons. Arthur stopped to have a look at the computers in the window. He was dead interested in computers, even though they were a hundred and fifty years beyond him.

"Amazing," he kept saying. "Amazing what they have these days. I was born a hundred and fifty years too early, that's my trouble."

"My trouble," I said to him, "isn't that I was *born* a hundred and fifty years too early, my trouble is that I *died* seventy years too early. That's *my* problem."

He gave me another of his when-you've-been-dead-as-long-as-I-have looks. "Harry," he said, "most people think they died too early." Then he looked back into Dixons' window. "I wish I had the money for a Game Boy," he said. "Or a Dreamcast. Or a Play Station."

"Come on, Arthur," I said impatiently. "I thought we were off to do a spot of haunting or something."

"In a minute," he muttered, and he went on staring into Dixons' window, dreaming about getting the latest gadgets for himself—anything, as long as it was digital.

As I waited for him to pry himself away from the display, who should come along but Norman Teel—Dave Teel's big brother. Dave Teel had been in the class above mine at school, and we used to play football together sometimes during break. He'd left school now, had big Norman, and had gone to work in a travel agent's.

I wasn't going to speak to him at first. What was the point, after all? But then sociability got the better of me, because I've always been the kind who likes a natter, and I find it hard not to say hello when I recognize someone.

So, "Hi, Norman," I said. "How are you doing?"

But instead of looking right through me like Mrs. Fraser had, he stopped and put his hand out and said, "Hello there, Harry, mate. How's it going these days?"

"Ahhhhhhh!"

Yes. I screamed. I screamed as loud as I could. Just as if I'd seen—

Well, a ghost.

"I haven't seen you for ages, Harry!" Norman went on. "What happened? I thought you must have died."

"I have," I tried to say.

"Where are you living now?" he asked.

"In the cemetery," I wanted to tell him. But I couldn't utter one ghostly word.

I just stood there, rooted to the spot, not knowing what to do. I was absolutely terrified. I mean, there I was, dead, and Norman was chatting away to me, just like I was still breathing.

It was like being haunted. And he wouldn't go away. He just stood there, nodding and smiling, like some kind of horrible fiend. I felt as if I was going mad. But then it all fell into place.

"I'm dead, too, Harry," he explained. "Didn't you realize? I went suddenly, just like that. It was something I picked up on holiday, some bug. Temperature of a hundred and four I had. And when I woke up, I wasn't alive anymore. I'm just down here tidying up a few loose ends, having a last walk down memory lane. But fancy seeing you here. I didn't know you'd passed on. It's a small world. Well, I must get on. Things to do. Have a good day."

And he was off. He strolled away, nodding to Arthur as he stood there, still drooling over the gadgets in the window.

I watched Arthur and I kept thinking about him, about what he'd done to the fruit machine, how he was able to manipulate things from—well—beyond the grave, and I wondered how far a thing like that could go.

Because to tell the truth, I had something in mind. You see, I had a scheme. There was something I was planning on, something I needed to do before I could ever be at peace with myself, before I would ever be able to make the journey to whatever lay beyond the Great Blue Yonder.

It was that unfinished business again, that thing I'd said to my sister, Eggy, the terrible thing I'd said about her being sorry when I was dead, and then going off and dying before we'd had a chance to patch things up.

I had to make my peace with Eggy before I could ever really say goodbye to the world and move on. And if I didn't, I'd just end up like Arthur, moping around the Other Lands, searching for someone he could never find, haunting his old haunts, moving among the living like a shadow of a shadow, like the ghost of a ghost.

But how could I ever say those words to her? How could I ever say, "Eggy, I'm sorry. Eggy, don't feel bad. Eggy, please forgive me for what I said to you before I stormed off, never to return." How could I when I had no words in me that any living person could hear?

I didn't even have the ghost of a chance.

And yet I had a plan. But to make it work, I needed to know how you did it, how you could switch things off and on and make them do what you wanted, like Arthur could.

If only I could control other things, the way I'd some-how made the leaf fall from the tree, the way I'd made Jelly's ballpoint leap from his hand. If I could do that, I could maybe pick up a pen and somehow make it write. If only I could still communicate with the living, if only I could say to Eggy all the things that were in my heart . . .

If only. If only.

If only I could have my time back to say a proper goodbye.

Maybe Arthur could explain to me how it all worked. Or maybe it was less a question of explaining and more a matter of trying it for yourself.

I turned to ask him. "Arthur," I said. "You know when you—"

But he was nowhere to be seen. I couldn't see him anywhere. And then I spotted him, perched halfway up a lamppost, sitting in a basket of flowers.

And he wasn't on his own. There was someone else sitting in another flower basket next to him.

"Wotcha!"

I looked up and half thought of saying "Wotcha yourself," but I didn't, because what I saw put it completely out of my mind.

There was another ghost up there, and going from the look of him, he must have been dead a good few years, at least. He wasn't exactly dressed in the latest fashion and had on one of those big, baggy suits that you see people wearing in news clips of the old days.

"Wotcha, Harry," Arthur repeated. "Come on up and join us."

The other ghost looked down at me.

"Yeah, come on up," he said, "room for a small one. There's another basket here, if you want it."

And seeing as I really had nothing else to do, I

hopped up and joined them on the lamppost, and the three of us sat there, lounging about in the swinging flower baskets, just like we were all on our holidays. Which maybe we were, if you can look on being dead as a holiday, which it might well be for some people.

The other ghost turned to Arthur and said, "Who's your mate?"

"This is Harry," Arthur said, introducing us. "And Harry, this is Stan."

We shook hands. That is we—well, you know what I mean.

"How are you, Harry?" Stan said. "Been dead long?"

"Seems like no time at all," I told him. "Though it's really been more like a few weeks."

Stan nodded, as if he quite understood. "I know just what you mean, mate," he said. "Time nips by like nobody's business. Yeah, it's amazing how the time flies when you're dead." Then he suddenly turned to Arthur and said, "Have you seen him yet?"

And Arthur said, "No," almost automatically, without even bothering to look around. "No, sorry, Stan, haven't seen him." And Stan looked a bit disappointed.

I sneaked a closer look at him. He was quite old, maybe seventy or so, maybe even older. Why he was up the lamppost, I'd no idea. I could only imagine that he had some unfinished business keeping him there and stopping him from crossing the Other Lands and heading for the Great Blue Yonder.

Arthur seemed to read my thoughts and to understand that a little explanation wouldn't go amiss.

"This is Stan's lamppost," he said. "Isn't it, Stan?"

"That's right," he nodded. "It is."

"He's been haunting it for years now, haven't you, Stan?"

"Yes," Stan agreed, "I have."

I didn't know quite how to respond, so I just nodded my head and said, "How interesting." I didn't think it was, though. I thought it was pretty stupid. I mean, of all the things you could come back and haunt, fancy haunting a lamppost. You could have haunted the cinema, or a nice stately home, or a five-star hotel.

So I could see the point in haunting somewhere comfortable, where there was a bit of entertainment, but why anyone would ever choose to haunt a lamppost, I couldn't think at all.

No, I'd definitely have gone for a cinema myself. In fact, the more I thought about it, the more I liked he idea. Because it was a big cinema, the one near us, really huge, with twelve different screens in it and new films every week. You could have spent your whole life— I mean, your whole death—in a place like that and never have got bored at all. And you could have got in to see all the films you're not supposed to see as well, all the ones for grownups, the ones with all the blood and gore and the swearing and the naughty bits in them.

I was sorely tempted to do it. If I hurried over there straightaway, I'd just be in time for the afternoon performance and I could get down to some serious haunting right away. But then I remembered Eggy and Mum and Dad and all my unfinished business, and I felt it wouldn't be right to spend the rest of eternity sitting in the multiplex cinema, watching all the latest releases until the time came when the cinema got so old they had to demolish it and I had to haunt somewhere else.

But a lamppost! I mean, why haunt a lamppost? Surely you could find somewhere a bit more interesting and a big less drafty than that. Not that Stan would really be feeling the draft, but all the same.

Stan raised his hands to shield his eyes and looked out over the plaza.

"Is that *him*, Arthur?" Stan said. "Is it him, at last?"

But Arthur just gave old Stan a bit of a look, as if he was totally crackers. "He'd be dead by now, Stan," Arthur said. "He'll be dead, too, remember. Dogs don't live as long as people. And if you've been a ghost for fifty years, then he definitely has to be, too. It's the ghost of a dog you should be looking for, not a real one."

But Stan didn't seem totally convinced.

"Not necessarily," he said. "He was always a very healthy dog. Very fit and active. He might still be alive. And he was only six when I passed on. So he'd only be fifty-six now. Which is no age at all for a dog, really. I'm sure there're plenty of dogs still around just as old as that."

"Only stuffed ones," Arthur said. Which was maybe a bit callous of him, even if it was the truth.

Stan stood up in the flower basket to get a better view of the terrier.

"Careful," I yelled at him as the baskets swayed in the wind. "Watch out! You'll have us all out! We'll all fall down and—"

And what? I didn't finish the sentence, and Stan ignored me, anyway.

"It's him, Arthur!" he said, getting more excited by the

second. "It's *him!* I'm *sure* it is! It's *definitely* him. It's Winston, I've found him at last!"

But just as he said it, a man dressed in raggedy clothes came round the corner, with a tin of beer in one hand and a bit of string in the other, which maybe served as the dog's lead. And he whistled to the dog and it ran after him, and they both went and sat down outside a shop, and the man put his cap on the pavement and started asking people if they could spare him some change.

Stan sat back down in the flower basket. His face looked sad and old and disappointed.

"No," he said. "Not him. Someone else's dog. Looked like him, though. It did look like Winston. Slightly different markings, though, now that I see him closer. Looked like him, though, very like him. I almost thought—well, never mind."

I felt a bit sorry for him, and I could tell that Arthur did, too.

"Hey, Stan," he said, "Harry and me were just thinking of popping back up to the Other Lands now for a while. Why don't you come with us? Have a break from looking for Winston. Get yourself a change of scenery. Why not, eh? Come on!"

But no.

"No, thanks," Stan said. "I'll stay here a while longer. He might turn up."

"But, Stan," Arthur said, "you've been haunting this lamppost for fifty years now. Don't you think that's long enough? I mean, if you haven't found Winston in fifty years, the chances are . . ."

Yes. Stan knew what the chances were. Who didn't?

But the thing was that I could have said the same to Arthur. I could have said, "Arthur, you've been looking for your mum for over a hundred years. If you haven't found her in a hundred years, the chances are . . ."

But that's always the way, isn't it? It's easy to be sensible for other people, but you can't always be sensible for yourself.

"No, I'll stay on here a bit," Stan said. "Thanks all the same, boys. But I'll just hang about a while longer. He might turn up."

"OK, then," Arthur said. "We'll probably see you again, then."

"More than likely," Stan agreed.

"Nice meeting you," I said. "I hope you find your dog."

"Me, too," he said. "Nice meeting you, Harry. See you around."

"Bye, then."

"Bye."

Arthur and I hopped down from the flower baskets and went on our way. I didn't really know what our way was, so I let Arthur go a bit in front, so that I could follow him and yet seem to be independent at the same time.

I looked back once, to see if Stan was still there. And there he was, halfway up the lamppost, sitting in his flower basket, scanning the plaza for signs of his long-lost dog. He seemed like a lookout on an old sailing ship, the kind you see pictures of in books, like a sailor up in the crow's-nest, and it seemed as though any minute he would shout "Thar she blows!" and the whole plaza would sail off in search of his long-lost dog.

Arthur quickened his pace. He seemed ever more anxious to return to the Other Lands and to resume the search for his mum. I had trouble keeping up with him and almost had to trot along behind him. There was no time now to ask him about how he had controlled the fruit machine. I felt annoyed with him for going so fast. But I was too proud to ask him to slow down, and I certainly didn't want to lose him, as I wasn't too sure how to get back to the Other Lands on my own. And I definitely didn't want to stay down here forever, a ghost among the living—I mean, what sort of a life is that?

We headed up the High Street. Arthur ran straight across the road. But I waited by the crossing for the little man in the sign to turn green. Safety first—that's me.

"Come on, Harry," Arthur called. "Don't hang about!" And on he went.

We strolled along the pedestrian walkway, went on through the park, and soon found ourselves on the path by the railway siding, the one that runs along by the back of the multiplex cinema.

I knew Arthur was in a hurry to get back and look for his mum, but all the same I couldn't resist it.

"Can you wait, Arthur? Just two minutes. Just while I look inside the cinema?"

He made a face but stopped just the same and said, "Yeah, all right. But get a move on, Harry."

"Coming in with me?" I said.

"No, thanks," he said. "Seen it before. I'll wait for you here. But just two minutes, mind. Don't start watching anything and getting interested in it and then forgetting what you're doing."

"I won't," I promised. "Two minutes, that's all."

And I went on inside.

The cinema foyer was all but deserted. Not packed, like you'd see it on a rainy Sunday afternoon. Two people were at the box office, waiting to buy tickets. The lady behind the ice cream counter was yawning. The man who ripped the tickets was leaning against the wall and chewing at one of his fingernails.

I went and looked at the list of what was playing. There was a new Walt Disney animation on, one that had just been released. It must have come out since I'd been dead. I decided to go and have a quick look at it, only for a second. I promised myself I wouldn't get too interested in it, as I'd told Arthur that I'd only be two minutes at the most.

I checked the screen number. Screen number eight, the board said, and the next performance was just about to start. I walked past the yawning lady and the man gnawing his fingernails, and I floated over the thick plush carpets until I got to the door of screen number eight. I went inside. It took a second for me to get used to the darkness. There was an advertisement up on the screen for a breakfast cereal. I looked around, not really expecting to find many people in there at that time of day.

But I was wrong. The cinema was packed to the gills and every single seat was taken. The cinema was completely full up—with ghosts.

They all but frightened the daylights out of me. To see them all in there. No people at all, just ghosts. Rows and rows of ghosts, all sitting there waiting for the film to start. It rattled your nerves. And it wasn't just that, it made me feel a bit sad, too, that there were so many people with so much unfinished business that they just couldn't leave the world behind them and move on to new things.

And I resolved right then that whatever else I did, I wouldn't become one of them. I just refused. I refused to turn into a sad old ghost who spent his mornings trying to put right his unfinished business and his afternoons sitting in the cinema with all the other ghosts, hoping that the latest film would take his mind off his troubles for a while.

I saw then that ghosts aren't really scary at all. They're more sad and misunderstood, if anything. But that wouldn't happen to me. I wouldn't let it. I was going to put things right with Eggy and say a proper goodbye to everyone and then I was going to see what lay beyond the Great Blue Yonder. I wouldn't be a sad ghost forever and ever. I just wouldn't. I refused.

As I stood there at the back of the cinema, the door opened behind me and two ladies came in along with two toddlers and a little girl of about five. All the ghosts turned round when they heard the creak of the door, and when they saw that some real live people were coming in, they let out a terrible moan—not that the people could hear it—and they started to complain like nobody's business.

"Oh, no!" a big fat ghost at the front said. "It's people! With children! They're the worst!"

"And they've got popcorn!" a second ghost moaned. "And sweets. With cellophane wrappers! I can't stand the crackle! The noise of it!"

"Those children will talk all through the film!" another

ghost whined. "And want to go to the toilet, right at the exciting bits! And they'll slurp their drinks! And—oh no! They're coming to sit on me now!"

I turned to go. I left them all in there, the two ladies with the three children and all the popcorn and sweets, with the hundreds of ghosts around them, muttering and moaning like a real load of sourpusses.

"I'm not going to get like that," I said to myself. "I'm not. Whatever happens." And I headed back out to find Arthur.

The last thing I heard, just as the film started, was the big fat ghost at the front of the cinema, turning round to complain about the sweet wrappers. "Oi!" he said. "Can't you keep those children quiet! There're ghosts in there trying to watch a film, you know! The least you could do is have a bit of consideration!"

It's people like that who give ghosts a bad name. They almost make you ashamed to be dead.

I didn't bother with the foyer this time, but walked straight out of the multiplex by going through the wall. There are some advantages to being dead—you can take a lot of shortcuts. I got outside, and there was Arthur, pretending to look at his watch.

"That was a *long* two minutes," he said dryly.

"Sorry, Arthur," I said. "I couldn't believe it. It was full of ghosts."

"Thought it would be," he said. "It usually is. It's why it's so chilly in there, too. They think it's the air-conditioning that keeps the place cool, but it isn't—it's the ghosts. Anyway, not to worry. We should be all right for getting back now. We're in luck. If we're quick, we should just about make it."

"Make what?" I said, wondering what he was talking about.

"That!" he said. "Over there. There was a shower of rain while you were in the cinema, and that always means a shortcut back to the Other Lands."

"So where do we go, then, Arthur?"

"Over there," he said. "Come on, quick, before it disappears."

And he ran toward it.

I could see it clearly now. It couldn't have been more than a hundred meters away. It seemed to glisten in the sunlight like a huge halo, full of wonderful shimmering colors, like in the patterns you might see in a kaleidoscope. It was the arc of a beautiful rainbow.

Home

"Just follow it up to the top," Arthur said. "That's all you have to do And then let go."

I didn't quite understand what he meant, and it must have shown on my face, because he added, "Don't worry about it, Harry. You'll know when you get there. Come on."

He headed for the rainbow, and I was about to follow him when something held me back. The great arc of the rainbow swept high above us, like the roof of some enormous cathedral.

"Come on, Harry," Arthur said, when he saw me hesitate. "Come on, I need to get back. I might find my mum. She might be wandering round by the Desk, right now, looking for a boy with a button."

But still I hesitated. I felt I couldn't go back. Not yet. I just couldn't. Not with all this unfinished business hanging over me. I felt I just had to try and settle it, right then and there. Or I'd be haunted by it forever, and never be at peace.

"You go without me, Arthur," I told him. "I'll wait for the next rainbow. I'll catch the next one."

He got a bit agitated then, as if he didn't like to leave me behind.

"Come on, Harry," he said. "Don't stay here. It's not the place for us, not for long. It's all right to visit, but you wouldn't want to live here."

"I *don't* want to live here," I said. "That's just it. I know I can't do that anymore. I just need to settle a bit of unfinished business, that's all. Just a couple of things I need to clear up. And as soon as I've done that, I'll be with you."

Arthur still held back, maybe thinking that he should offer to stay with me while I got my unfinished business settled. The rainbow behind him started to fade, and I urged him to grab a ride on it, quick, before it was completely gone. But still he hesitated.

"You *sure* you'll be all right, Harry?"

"Of course I will. I can look after myself."

"Something might happen to you."

"What?" I said. "What can happen to me now? I'm dead, aren't I, Arthur? Everything else has got to be an improvement."

Arthur looked at me a moment longer, then he shrugged and sort of gave up on me and said, "All right, then, Harry, if you're sure. But if anything goes wrong, well—it's your funeral."

"Yeah," I said, "I know."

He grinned then, and I grinned back. Then he waved and said, "See you, then. See you up there, maybe."

"OK, Arthur," I said. "And thanks. Thanks for helping

me and for looking out for me. It's a bit of a shock at first when you wake up and find yourself dead. It's nice to have someone to sort of explain things to you and show you around a bit."

"No problem," he said. "I'd better go, then, the rainbow's vanishing. If I wait any longer I'll—"

And with that he jumped up and just caught the tail of the rainbow as it began to fade. I watched as he seemed to fly along the curve of it, up to its highest point, up to the apex. And then he vanished in a twinkle of light, and he was gone, back to the Other Lands. And I was alone. And I felt alone. More alone than I'd ever felt before.

I felt suddenly cold inside. I wished I had some kind of ghostly coat to wrap around me. I felt cold and lonely and almost wanted to cry. And it was the first time I'd really felt like that since I'd been dead.

But I knew that whatever these feelings were, I couldn't give in to them. I had to keep a grip on myself and not go to pieces. Because a ghost isn't much use to anyone at the best of times, but a ghost who's cracked up and gone to pieces is no use at all.

I watched for a moment as the rainbow faded from the sky. One second it was there, in all its glory, the next it had disappeared. It was time for me to go, too. So I turned and I began to make my way back to the city. And I knew just where I was headed.

I was going home.

Now that Arthur wasn't with me, I seemed to have more time for my thoughts. You know how it is when a friend's with you, sometimes you feel you have to say something, even when there's really nothing to say, just to keep the conversation going, and so's they won't think you're boring.

But when you're on your own, you don't have to think of what to say next. You can just let the thoughts come into your mind, however they will. It's almost like having a bar of chocolate all to yourself, that you don't have to share with anyone.

So I walked back through the plaza. There was Stan, still up the lamppost, still sitting in the flower basket, scanning the streets for a sign of his long-lost dog, Winston.

"Any luck, Stan?" I called to him as I went by, just to be polite.

"No," he said. "Not yet. But I've got the feeling that today I'm going to be lucky." (Though I had the feeling that he had that feeling every day.) "Where's your mate?" he asked. "You on your own now?"

"Caught the last rainbow," I explained. "Gone back up."

"Ah," Stan said. "I see. Right." And he turned away from me then, and went back to looking out for his dog. That seemed to end the conversation, so I continued on my way, thinking my private thoughts.

There were a lot of them, too. All sorts of bits and pieces came into my mind. Like what might happen to you once you made it to the Great Blue Yonder, what would lie in store for you there and what you could expect, and whether it was something to be afraid of or not so bad at all.

I didn't really think of where I was going, or of which direction to take. My feet just seemed to know the way, and they carried me along like I was a passenger on a train and they were a set of wheels.

I found myself going by the cathedral, and I looked up at the clock. Quite a bit of time had passed since Arthur and I had come down from the Other Lands. It was getting on for half past three now. Eggy would be coming out of school. Mum would be making her way home from her part-time job. Dad worked flexi-time and you never knew what he'd be doing. He might be at work, or he might have accumulated enough hours to let him take the afternoon off. He liked to do that sometimes. To be able to get out when everyone else was working.

On I went. The schools were emptying. The streets filled up with kids. Kids with lunch boxes, kids with satchels, kids in uniforms, kids in jeans and sneakers.

A ghostly lump came to my ghostly throat. I felt angry and sad and bitter and tearful all at once. For the first time since I'd been dead I wanted to shout and scream and rage and yell out, "It's not *right!* It's not *fair!* I want my life back! I was only a kid, I shouldn't have had to die. It's all that stupid truck's fault. It wasn't even as if I was to blame. It's not as if I even *deserved* it! It's so unfair!"

But then I thought, Well, who *does* deserve it? Who does deserve to have bad things happen to them? Nobody, really. And I suppose that things just happened whether you deserve them or not.

It isn't fair, though, I thought as I watched all the children go by. They walked around me and through me, laughing and messing about, fighting even, some of them, or just talking to their mates, having some fun and larking around.

I so wanted to be alive again. I can't tell you how much. I so, so wanted to be alive. I so wanted to be one of them. And all the ordinary things which I'd always taken for granted—just little things, like being able to kick a football or being able to eat a bag of crisps—how I missed them.

And how I envied them. How I envied all those children their lives. Oh, I knew they weren't *all* happy. I knew some of them were miserable or sad or getting bullied or worried about their exams or had trouble at home or were just plain unhappy—but still I envied them, even the unhappy ones. It's true. I did. I even envied them their unhappiness. Because at least they were alive. And I wasn't.

Maybe this was why Arthur hadn't wanted to leave me down here on my own. Maybe this was what happened to you. It wasn't that anyone else was a danger to you—you were a danger to yourself. It was what was inside you that was so dangerous and upsetting. It was you.

I walked on. I tried to ignore them, all the children passing by me. I kept my eyes down and stared at the footpath as I cut through the park. I could hear the sound of a football game, I could hear the squeak of the unoiled swings, I could hear the sounds of bikes riding by, I could hear the chimes of the ice cream van, I could hear—I could hear the voices and the laughter and—

Never mind. Never mind.

I kept my eyes down, following the narrow strip of asphalt which snaked through the park and which wound around the back of the gardens, and which eventually took you through the old churchyard and ultimately to the lane at the back of my house.

The voices receded, the chimes of the ice cream van were farther away. The chimes grew fainter as the van drove off in search of other hot and thirsty children who needed cooling down in other recreation grounds.

I looked up. Safe now. I was out of the park. I was somewhere else. Somewhere I wouldn't feel myself to be quite such a sore thumb. Or so sad at being alone.

I was in the cemetery.

I walked slowly through it, going along by the graves, reading, as ever, the inscriptions on the stones. I always used to look for the oldest and the youngest ages. I don't know why. Just curiosity, I suppose.

Then suddenly I stopped, and the thought came to me, "What about *my* grave? This is where I'll be buried, won't it?" And I left the path and hurried to the upper end of the cemetery where all the new plots were. I found the latest row and went along it, and there I was, fourth from the end.

There I was. There I *really* was. And they hadn't half done me proud. You should have seen it! Well, you still *can* see it if you ever go there. They'd gone and got me this fantastic headstone. Probably granite, it was, or maybe polished marble. But it was such a nice color, a kind of warm reddish brown, with an autumn kind of feel to it. You could even have made jewelry out of it, it was that nice a stone. And there was a design on it, too, around the edges, a bit sort of curly but nothing too fancy, just nice and simple. And there was my name and the date I was born, and the date when the truck got me. And then there was a short inscription from everyone at home, saying how much they'd loved me, and how they always would, and how they'd miss me always. And there, sunk into the earth by the foot of the grave, was a little container for flowers, and it was full of red roses, 'cause red had always been my favorite color.

And there, tending to the flowers, there—

There was my dad.

What can I say? I can't describe it, really, so maybe there's no point in my even trying. But I'll tell you this: when you're alive and someone dies, you feel so upset that you'll never see them again, it's just awful. But when you're a ghost, and when you *do* see someone again, but when you know that they can't see *you* and that you can't talk to them, or ever walk down the road holding their hand, or have a game of football with them, or a muck—about with them, or ever put your arms around them ever again . . .

It makes you feel pretty bad, too.

And that's how I felt, pretty bad. And I'll say no more than that.

We stood there for a while, my dad and me, him staring at my headstone and me staring at him, and both of us feeling pretty bad. Then eventually he looked at his watch and decided that he had to go, and he said, "Bye, then, Harry." And I said, "Hello, Dad," though obviously he couldn't hear me.

Then he said, "I'll come again tomorrow, Harry, same as usual," And at that—wanting to spare him from getting so upset every day—I said, "It's all right, Dad. Don't feel you have to come here every day. Once a week will be fine, Dad, honest. Or once a month, even. Or just come and see me on my birthday. I won't mind. That'll be fine, Dad, really. Or if you want to go off on holiday and can't get here for a while, I'll understand. Or you could send Mrs. Morgan from next door along instead, if you want to. I'll understand. I'd rather you did it that way, Dad, than get upset all the time."

But of course he couldn't hear me.

"Bye, Harry," he said. "Bye."

And he turned on his way and walked up the cemetery path. I ran to catch up with him. He wasn't going very quickly, not like he usually did, not sort of bouncing along all cheerful and swinging his arms. Quite the contrary. He just shuffled along, his arms by his sides, lost in whatever he was thinking.

"Hang on, Dad!" I shouted. "I'll come with you."

On he went, heading for home. I soon caught up with him. And, you know, the way I felt, you'd have thought it was *him* who'd died, not *me*.

"Are you off home now, Dad?" I said. I assumed he was. Where else would he be going? "We can go together," I suggested.

On he went. I reached out and took his living hand with my ghostly one. And we walked along the path together, hand in hand, me and my dad.

Recently, just before my accident, I'd started feeling that I was getting a bit big to be seen out holding my dad's hand. You know—the way you do. Same as when you don't want your mum to kiss you anymore, or at least not while other people are looking. But I didn't feel like that then. I didn't care who saw me. I didn't care if the whole world saw me out holding my dad's hand. I only wished they could. I only wished I could.

I didn't bother waiting for Dad to open the door when we got home, I just walked in straight through it and immediately headed for the kitchen, where Mum would more than likely be getting the tea on, and where Eggy would be, still in her school uniform, stuffing her face with biscuits.

And right enough, the instant I came in through the wall, I found them there. But you should have seen them. Talk about miserable! You'd think that somebody had died. In fact, for a moment there, I maybe thought that somebody *had* died. Somebody else, that is, not me. Maybe Alt the cat had died from grief at me not coming back from my bike ride. I hoped he hadn't. I'd have been really upset about that. I mean, I know he was only a cat, but all the same you can get very attached to your pets. You only had to look at Stan up his lamppost to see that. Not that *you'd* be able to see him, though, not even with 3-D specs.

But then Dad opened the door and came in, and they both looked up at him. No "Hello," no "Had a good day?" no "Is the traffic bad?" no "Did you get a paper?" no nothing. Just a look. A look each. And Dad nodded to them and said, "I went round," and then he sat at the table.

"I went round myself this morning," Mum said.

"I went round on my way back from school," Eggy said. "I must have just missed you."

"Yes," Dad said. "You must."

And then the three of them just sat there, looking like a wet week at the seaside. In fact, they looked so miserable, I almost left. I mean, I'm not saying that they're all a great cheery bunch up in the Other Lands, but there's miserable and there's *miserable*. And say what you like about Arthur, at least you could have a bit of a laugh with him, even if he had been dead for a hundred and fifty years.

But this lot—you wouldn't believe it. Faces *that* long! Expressions *that* miserable! It was enough to get anyone down, seeing the three of them sitting at the kitchen table looking like they were all about to top themselves.

I had to do something to cheer them up. Only what? I sat down on my old chair and wondered what I could do to take their mind off things. Then I got it.

"I know," I said. "Let's have a game of Monopoly!"

Nothing. No response at all. They just sat there as if they hadn't heard a word.

"OK," I said, trying again, "how about Scrabble?"

Nothing. They looked right through me.

"Trivial Pursuit, then?" I suggested. "Me and Dad against Mum and Eggy. That all right? OK. You lot wait here, then, and I'll go and get the box."

No. Not a flicker. Not a blink. I might as well have been dead. Well, yeah, I was, I know, but what I mean is—oh, never mind. I'm not going into all that again. You'll find out for yourselves sometime. Let's just leave it at that.

Well, I didn't know what to do. How could I cheer them up? What could I say? What was there? I couldn't even make them a cup of tea. All I could do was to stand there, haunting the kitchen, an invisible presence.

Then I had an idea. Not for cheering them up, but

on a different matter. It was another of my brain waves, really. What I thought was that I could haunt the place *forever!* Move back in, on a permanent basis, and it would be just like old times. I could have my old room back, and life could go on as before and things would be the same as ever—the only real difference would be that I was dead. But that didn't mean that we couldn't go on living together. We could be a family again. Me and Mum and Dad and Eggy. And if I could somehow make myself visible to them, they'd be able to see me just like I could see them. And we could still do things together; we'd just have to warn people in advance, and be a bit careful, that was all. Like, if we went to the zoo, when Dad got the tickets, instead of asking for two adults and two children and one old-age pensioner, if we brought Gran along, he'd just need to ask for two adults, one child, one old-age pensioner and a ghost. I was sure they'd have a category for ghosts. Or maybe they'd even let you in for free, as long as you didn't spook the animals.

I was sure it would work. It would be OK. And when we went out for meals, I could just sit and watch them eat. I wouldn't mind, as long as I was there.

And yet, on reflection, I wasn't so sure. Not sure at all. Not when I thought about Eggy growing up and Mum and Dad getting older and the years going by and me always the same. Older, but no older, a boy forever, like Peter Pan.

No, I thought, that would be too sad, I wouldn't be able to bear it. I mean, to be a dead person for the rest of your life, what sort of an existence was that? And anyway, who'd want to spend the next fifty years or so with a miserable lot like this?

"I think I'll go up to my room," Eggy said. "Maybe read for a while."

"OK, Tina," Mum said (they all called her that apart from me.) "I'll start the tea in a bit." And she sort of patted Eggy on the shoulder, and Eggy patted her hand in return, and she went over and gave Dad a kiss on the head and patted him, too. Then she went up to her room. They'd obviously taken up patting each other in quite a big way since I'd been gone. They never used to pat each other before. Not a lot.

I was on my way to follow Eggy up to her room and to try and somehow settle the unfinished business when Dad turned to Mum and said, "You know," he said, "I wonder sometimes if maybe we should have had more children. Maybe it wouldn't be so bad, then, somehow, maybe it would be easier to bear. Maybe—do you think?"

But Mum just gave him a sad sort of smile, and she reached across the table and took his hand and said, "You know it wouldn't have made any difference, Bob. It wouldn't have mattered if we'd had a hundred children. We'd still miss Harry just as much, every single little bit as much. You know we would."

"Yes," he nodded. "I know. You're right. No one could ever replace Harry. No one. He was a one-off. He was such a character. I know I got mad with him sometimes, but he did make me laugh. I did love him. I miss him so much."

And there were tears in Dad's eyes and tears in Mum's and she said, "Me, too, me, too, I miss him so much, too." And then she pulled her chair around the table so she was sitting next to Dad, and she put her arm around him, and he put his arm round her—and they both started to cry.

I felt that bad. I don't mind telling you. I had to do something to stop it, it was that upsetting.

"How about a game of I-Spy?" I shouted as loud as I could. "It'll take our minds off it for a while and then we'll all feel better!"

But my shouting was as silent as the tomb, and a bit more silent on top.

"How about doing the crossword, then," I said. "The difficult one. It'll give us all something else to think about. Probably keep us occupied for hours."

I thought this at them as hard as I could, with that really tightly squeezed sort of thinking, when you scrunch your thoughts up as hard as you possibly can. Maybe it did the trick, or maybe they just got fed up with being miserable. Either way, Mum went and got the kitchen roll and they had a bit each to blow their noses on, and then another bit for dabbing at their eyes. Then Mum got all sort of busy and businesslike, as she did when she'd made her mind up about something, and she went to the fridge and said, "Well, this won't do. I'd better get the tea on. Want to or not, we still have to eat."

And Dad pulled himself together and bucked up a bit, too, and he said, "I'll maybe go out, run the lawnmower over that lawn." And Mum gave him a look at first and then nodded and said, "Yes, why don't you do that, Bob? That would be a good idea."

So out Dad went to mow the back garden lawn. Though you could see it certainly didn't need mowing. The whole garden was practically bald. He must have been out there mowing it every night. There was as much sense in him going out mowing that lawn as there was in a fish turning up at the barber's and asking for a haircut. But he went and did it anyway, and I'm sure he had his reasons.

"Hello, Mum," I said, now that I was left on my own in the kitchen with her. "It's Harry, Mum, come back to visit you." It felt so strange to be there alone with her, watching her put the spuds on, and her not able to see me. "I'm a ghost now, Mum," I said. "I know you can't hear me, but I can't just stand here and not talk to you. I have to say something, or else I'll just feel like a right lemon."

She went and got the fish fingers out from the freezer compartment.

"Thanks for the nice headstone, Mum," I said. "It's a lovely color. I hope you didn't spend too much on it. Though, then again, on the other hand, you won't need to give me any pocket money now, so maybe that'll help a bit, to, you know, defray expenses or whatever it is and stuff."

I regretted saying that immediately. I was glad then that she couldn't hear me. I knew she'd have given all the pocket money in the world and all the wages, too, just to have me back and give me a cuddle. And so would I. So I was sorry I'd said that. It was stupid. It had just come out. I hadn't meant it.

I thought of Eggy again, and of what I'd said to her. And what she'd said to me just before I'd set off on my bike. Only we *had* heard each other that time. And that was why I'd returned, why I'd come back—as they say— from the grave.

"I'm just going to go up and see Eggy now, Mum," I said, as she put the peas in a pan. I'll come back and see you before I go. OK?"

She went and got the knives and forks and started to lay the table. She laid four places. Yeah, that's right. One, two, three, *four*. And she put out four glasses, too, for the drinks. Then she remembered that I wasn't there—at least not in any way that she could know me. And she muttered, "Oh, no, I've done it again," like she was always doing it and that it made her angry with herself.

She looked out of the window to the back garden, where my dad was going up and down mowing the lawn with no grass, like she was glad he hadn't seen her mistake, or it would only set him off again. She went and took my knife and fork away and put them back in the drawer, and she put my glass away in the cupboard. Then she stood there and looked straight at me, almost as if she could really see me, and she said, "Oh, Harry. Oh, Harry. Oh, Harry."

And I said, "Oh, Mum. Oh, Mum." And I ran to her and put my arms around her and hugged her as tight as I could.

Only I couldn't. And nor could she. So she went back to making the tea. And I left her in the kitchen, and I went on up to Eggy's room, to try and somehow make my peace with her, to somehow forgive her and be forgiven. And then I wouldn't have to be a restless ghost anymore. I wouldn't have to stalk the earth or live up a lamppost in a basket of flowers or spend my days in the multiplex cinemas, moaning at the living whenever they came in to see the films.

I could be at peace. I could move on to—to who knew where? To a new life, maybe? To some different kind of existence. To whatever lay beyond the horizon of the Other Lands. To the shores of the Great Blue Yonder.

Upstairs

The stairs didn't creak like they usually did. And the number of times I'd cursed them for that. It would always happen just when I was planning on getting Eggy and was working on something really sneaky. And there I'd be, tiptoeing up toward her room with a nasty surprise for her, when *Creeeeek!* I'd put my foot on that floorboard and it would give the whole game away.

But this time, nothing. Not a sound. Just the faint crackle of music coming from Eggy's room. She always had her radio on, even when she wasn't really listening to it. She just kept it on, soft and low, as a kind of background to her thoughts or to whatever she was doing.

On I went, up the stairs. I realized that I was tiptoeing, from force of habit. I stopped and walked normally, heavily even, stomping my feet down onto the stairs—but of course, they didn't make a sound.

I was on the landing now. I remembered how the carpet used to feel as you walked on it barefoot from the bathroom to your bedroom. I remembered how it tickled the bottoms of your toes, as you dashed to get your pajamas on and as you heard Eggy shouting, "I can see your willy!" and rude stuff like that. And you'd tell her to belt up and be quiet and threaten to get her next time—whenever that was.

Of course the carpet didn't tickle now, but with an effort of memory, I could almost bring the feeling back. And yet with each step, it seemed to get a little harder to recall the feel of the rough wool in between your toes. Yes, step by step it was getting harder and harder to remember what it had felt like to be alive.

Eggy's door was closed. But her usual sign wasn't up there. It had been there so long that the paint on the rest of the door had faded around it, leaving this little whiter-than-white patch in the shape of a square.

She'd put the notice up after I'd walked into her room once too often without knocking. She'd spent a couple of hours on it, putting a squiggly border around it and doing it in her best handwriting.

The notice had read:

On no account whatsoever enter this room without knocking. This especially applies to all boys. Especially any boy going under the name of Harry. Improperly dressed callers will be refused admittance. No jeans. No sneakers. No stupid little brothers. Ties must be worn at all times. Enter this room without permission and you DIE!

Signed, the management

So she went and put the notice on the door, then, and so to retaliate I went and put one up on mine. And my notice said:

GET LOST PIG-FACE. YOU CAN'T COME IN. THIS APPLIES TO SISTERS ONLY.

But the only trouble was that Eggy didn't want to come into my room much, so it was no real hardship for her to stay out of it, so I wasn't gaining anything by forbidding her to enter. And my mum made me take the sign down, anyway, as she said "pig-face" was rude. But she let Eggy keep her sign up, which I didn't think was fair.

So I soon got bored after that, especially as I couldn't go into Eggy's room to annoy her anymore and I had to find some other way to keep myself amused. So what I did was to keep knocking on her door in all these different outfits to ask if I was properly dressed to come in yet.

The first time I went in my Halloween mask. The next time I went with nothing on at all. The third time I went with my swimming trunks on over my head and wearing Mum's old slippers, the ones that look like big fluffy bananas. The fourth time I knocked, Eggy just shouted at me to get lost without even opening the door. And the fifth time I went to call, I saw another line had been added to the notice on the door. It said, "Harrys will not be admitted under any circumstances whatsoever. Harrys who persistently knock at this door will get their teeth loosened and will be given a punch in the gob to play with. Thank you for your cooperation, the management."

So I didn't bother knocking then, and decided to leave things to cool off for a while.

Eggy did start letting me back into her room after a time, but the sign always stayed up on the door, sort of like a caution, I suppose, a warning that I was there only under sufferance. But the notice wasn't there now. She must have taken it down. She probably felt bad about that line in it—"Enter this room without permission and you die."

And you know, it's a funny thing, but when people annoy you all the time, you wish more than anything that they'd just buzz off and leave you alone. And then one day they *do* buzz off and they *do* leave you alone, but instead of feeling pleased about that, sometimes all you feel is lonely.

Still, door closed or door open, door locked or door unlocked, it was all the same to me. There was nothing that could keep me out of anywhere now. I could walk into the vault of the Bank of England and admire all the gold if I wanted. Not that I could have done much with it, but isn't that always the way? By the time your dreams come true, they're not your dreams anymore, and you're already dreaming of something else.

So I made my way along the landing, a plan half forming in my mind, but then, as I passed the door to my bedroom, I couldn't resist the impulse to just pop inside and see the old place again, and see what had changed. So I walked in through the door.

Nothing. Nothing had changed. Nothing except that it was tidy now. So tidy you'd know immediately that nobody could possibly have lived there. It was people-are-coming-to-visit tidy, we're-trying-to-sell-the-house tidy. It was your mother's dream of tidy, just like she was always nagging you to keep it.

My clothes had all been put away. They were hanging in the wardrobe and folded up in the drawers. My magazines and comics were neatly stacked in a pile under the chair. All my books and annuals had been put away in the bookcase, all in order, from big to small, all the right way up, and all with their spines facing outward so that you could read the titles and the author's names.

My bed was made. My Warhammer pieces were all in their box. My pens were in the jar. My football posters were still on the wall, only the peeling edges had been stuck back up with fresh blobs of Blu-Tack. Yes, it was all there—apart from me. It was like a car without a driver. I thought, like an airplane without a pilot. What use was a room with nobody in it?

I didn't stay long. I wouldn't let myself remember everything that had once been me and that had once been mine. I tried not to think of all the good days and the happy times I'd spent in my room. Sometimes I maybe had a friend over and we were making a model, or playing a game, or just talking. Most of the time I was on my own there. But that was OK. That's what your own room's supposed to be—a place to be alone in when you want to be, or need to be. But I didn't want to be there on my own just then, so I walked back out through the door and straight into—

Alt!

I know, it's an odd name for a cat—and that's the abbreviated version. His real name was Alternative, but as that was a bit of a mouthful, we called him Alt for short. It was my dad who thought the name up. Eggy and I had been arguing for ages over what to call this kitten, and Dad got so fed up with all the shouting and disagreeing and the stupid suggestions that he looked up from the computer where he'd been tapping away at something and shouted, "OK! That's it! We're going to call him Alternative! And no more arguing!"

And that was that.

I expect he must have got the idea from the computer keyboard. He probably just looked down at it, saw the Alt key, and that was it—Alternative.

So it was an odd name, but it stuck. And it could have been worse. He might have called the cat Numerical or Page Up or Scroll Lock or System Requirements or Caps Lock or Delete or something. But that was how it all came about.

Anyway, I walked out through my bedroom wall to find myself face to face with Alt—well, not face to *face*, exactly, but shin to whiskers. I hadn't expected to find him there, and for a second I froze. But that was nothing as to what *he* did. He didn't just freeze, he turned to ice. He went rigid, and as he did so, all his fur stood on end, just like he'd been plugged in to an electrical outlet. And I thought about the electric chair in America, and wondered if maybe they had an electric cat basket as well, to put an end to vicious cats who'd been terrorizing society.

"Hello, Alt," I said. "Have you missed me?"

I bent down to stroke his fur and to maybe try and calm him a little. I knew I wouldn't be able to *really* stroke him, but my memory of stroking him was still vivid enough in my mind for it to be almost like the real thing.

But as I crouched down and reach out to touch him, his fur bristled up even higher, and his back arched so much that he almost turned into a black-and-white question mark.

"It's OK, Alt," I said. "It's only me. How are you? Don't be afraid. It's just Harry."

His fur was standing up so much now and looking so brittle and spiky that he almost seemed like a scrubbing brush.

"It's OK, Alt, it's Harry," I said. "I'm just dead at the moment, that's all, good cat . . ."

I directed these comforting words at him, but they didn't seem to calm him down. I thought they might, because he was obviously a sensitive cat. After all, for the whole day I'd stood right next to people I used to know—even *sat* on them, in some cases, even held their hands, like I did with Dad, or hugged and cuddled them, like I did with Mum—and yet not one of them had realized that I was there, or had any inkling at all.

But Alt did. Mind you, I'd heard that about animals, plenty of times—that they have some kind of sixth sense. And people say that they often know in advance when storms and earthquakes are about to arrive, even when the earthquake could be hours away and storms yet to blow up.

"Come on, Alt," I said. "Come on, it's only Harry, it's only me."

I reached out for him. I saw that his claws were unsheathed. His teeth were bared, too, just like he was a little lion out to kill a little zebra.

"Alt, come on—it's Harry."

He began to hiss, sounding something like a leaking water pipe. I decided that it might be best to leave him alone, and I started to back off, but maybe I moved away too quickly because he suddenly let out the most blood-curdling, stomach-churning, eardrum-shattering screech you've ever heard. He all but cracked every mirror in the house. And then, not content with doing it once, he went and did the same thing again.

"Meowoooooooooeeeee!"

It was awful.

I'd heard him sometimes out in the garden at night, when he'd meet up with another cat and they'd get a duet going, but that was nothing compared to this. I mean, sometimes my dad would even come into my room to borrow my water pistol, my one-hundred-foot-range Super Soaker, and he'd fill it up with water and take pot shots from the bathroom window at Alt and whoever else was in the choir. And my mum would be saying to him, "You shouldn't do that, it's cruelty to animals," and he'd say, "What about *them* and the noise *they're* making? It's cruelty to eardrums." And then he'd add, "Besides, it's only water. A drop of water never hurt anyone." And then he'd take aim with the Super Soaker and—*splatt!*

End of performance.

But that was nothing compared to this. This was like a hundred babies all crying at once while seven hundred sirens went off and while two thousand teachers dragged twenty thousand fingernails down four thousand black-boards.

It was *awful*.

Eggy's door burst open.

"Alt! What are you doing? Why are you making that horrible noise!"

Then Mum and Dad came out of the kitchen and looked up the stairs.

"Eggy! What's going on? What's wrong with that cat?"

So there they are, all looking at Alt, and there's Alt howling and staring at me, looking like he's about to spring up at any moment and get me by the throat. And I somehow felt like I'd gone and got myself into trouble again. And all I could think to do was to sort of wave feebly at everyone and say, "Hello, Mum, hello, Dad, hello, Eggy. It's only me."

Alt backed into a corner and looked ready to fight to the last clump of fur. Dad came up the stairs to see him.

"Come on, Alt, what's the matter, old fellow? You look like you've seen a ghost."

And he wasn't far wrong there, either. Dad reached out to try and calm him, but Alt just swatted at his hand with his paw full of open claws.

"Ow!"

Dad looked down at his fingers. There were four weals along the length of his hand, and one of them was already bleeding.

"You'll need to wash that," Mum said.

"I know!" Dad snapped at her.

"And disinfect it."

"I know," he said, and he went into the bathroom to wash the wound under the tap. Then he got an antiseptic wipe and cleaned the scratches with it, and he cursed a bit as it stung. Then he wrapped his hand up in toilet paper while Mum found him a bandage.

"Have you had a tetanus injection recently?" she asked him.

"Yes!" he said, still a bit snappy.

"What about rabies?" Mum said.

"*Rabies!* How can he have *rabies?*"

"Well, you know," Mum said, "mad cat disease or something."

"*Mad cat disease?*"

"From eating infected pet food or something."

"He can't have mad cat disease," Dad said. "There's no such *thing* as mad cat disease—is there?" he added, a bit uncertainly.

They both turned and looked at Alt then, who was still making his last stand in the corner, ready to fight everyone and everything to death.

"He certainly looks a bit crackers," Mum said.

"Maybe he's had a breakdown?" Eggy suggested. She was standing in the doorway of her room, giving Alt plenty of space and not wanting to get too near to him and frighten him even more.

Dad looked at Eggy.

"Breakdown?" he said. "The cat's having a breakdown? If anyone's having a breakdown round here, I am. I'm having a breakdown, that's who's cracking up—me. Never mind the cat!"

And just after he said that, and just as I went to pat him on the back and say, "Take it easy, Dad, it can't be that bad," Alt must have seen me move, because he let out another of his terrible wails. And if we'd thought the other ones were bad, well, this was even worse. This was the wail to end all wails. And I wasn't just worried about him cracking the mirrors now, I thought he might well go and crack all the bricks, too, and the whole house would fall down. And I felt that maybe I should never have come back to see them all, that I was the cause of this, and I was just bringing them trouble.

The dead and the living don't mix, I thought. They just don't have anything in common anymore. We'd had a parting of the ways—only instead of keeping going, I'd come back to retrace my steps. And maybe I shouldn't have done it. And I wouldn't have, either, if it hadn't been for the unfinished business.

It was Eggy who came to the rescue.

"You know, Dad," she said, "I think that if you gave Alt a clear run out, he'd be OK. He's cornered in there and can't see any way of escaping from whatever it is. He just needs some space."

"Yes, but what's 'whatever it is,' Tina? Why's he gone like this?"

"Oh, you know cats, Dad. They have funny turns all the time. Just go back down the stairs and open the door for him and he'll be OK."

"OK. Come on," Mum said, "let's try it."

So they went down the stairs and they opened the front door, and then they backed away from the door so that there was nothing to block his exit, and Eggy looked at Alt, and she pointed at the open door, and she said, "OK, Alty. It's clear now. Off you go."

I'd like to say he didn't need asking twice, but he did. He needed asking several times, and he still wouldn't move.

I realized then that it was because I was standing in his way, and to get down the stairs he first had to run through me, which he plainly didn't want to do. So I stood to one side, to give him a clear way, and I waved my hand to beckon him on and said, "OK, Alt. There you go."

And that did it.

There was one more of those awful wails, which must have curdled all the milk in the fridge—if not all the milk in the local supermarket, and that was over a mile away— and then Alt was off, just like he was in the Olympics and the starting pistol had been fired. And there he was, going for the gold, all the way down the stairs and straight out of the front door. Then he was off across the gardens and soon out of sight, and I wouldn't have been surprised to learn that he'd ended up in Australia.

"Oh, well, he'll be back," Dad said, his head poking out of the door. "He'll be back sooner or later, I daresay."

And he closed the front door and went back to the kitchen.

Mum hesitated a moment and glanced up the stairs to where Eggy was looking down. Their eyes met, and they both seemed to be saying something without actually needing to say anything, as if looks spoke volumes, just like poets and pop songs say they do.

"You all right, Tina?"

"I'm OK, Mum. Are you OK?"

"I'm all right. Tea'll be ready soon. I'll call you."

"OK, Mum."

"OK."

And they gave each other a pale, wan kind of smile,

and Mum headed for the kitchen and Eggy headed for her room, and I walked in right behind her, before she had the chance to close the door.

Of course, I could have walked in, anyway. But the novelty of walking through walls and closed doors soon wears off, and you want to do things the ordinary way again and to be like everyone else. You don't always want to be going through closed doors like you had to sneak in everywhere. Sometimes it's nice to go in through an open one, and feel welcome.

Eggy

Eggy's room was always tidy. Not like mine. My mum claimed it was because girls are just naturally tidy and boys aren't. But I don't think so. I've seen girls who were like walking garbage bags. I've even seen some girl's bedrooms that looked like a garbage truck had exploded in them.

Pete Salmas showed me his sister's room once when I was round at his house on a sleepover.

"Come and see this, Harry," he'd said. "You've got to see it to believe it."

Well, he was right about that. For a start, you could hardly get the door open for all the junk. And when you finally did get your head round for a peek at the place, well, it was unbelievable. It was just like his sister had turned into a bag lady. There was stuff everywhere. Comics, papers, magazines, posters of the latest heart-throb with *I love you* messages written on them in lipstick. There was underwear on the floor and pairs of tights hanging out of drawers, looking like a load of cobwebs.

"She won't mind us looking, will she, Pete?" I asked him. "I mean, she not *in* here, is she?"

And he just shrugged and said, "How would you know?"

And he was right about that. How *would* you know? She could have been in there even as we were sneaking a look inside, buried under a heap of old T-shirts, and no one would ever have been able to tell.

"What about your mum, Pete?" I said. "Doesn't she get mad?"

"Used to," he said. "All the time. But then she gave up. She said if Poppy—" (that was his sister's name) "—if Poppy couldn't be bothered to keep her own room tidy at her age, then my mother certainly wasn't going to do it for her anymore. So that's how it's ended up—deadlock."

The radio was murmuring away in the background. I never knew how Eggy could work with the radio always on. But she did. Even when she did her homework it was on and the music would still be playing. And sometimes my dad would come in and say, "How can you work with that racket? How can you concentrate? Doesn't it distract you?"

And Eggy would say, "Dad, the only thing distracting me is you coming in and asking me why the radio isn't distracting me. OK?"

And he'd go off then and leave her to it. But he'd come back a bit later and say the same thing all over again.

So the radio was softly murmuring, and I heard the

DJ's voice as he introduced the new number one. And you know, I hadn't heard it before. Hadn't even *heard* it—the new number-one record on the charts. And once again I had the feeling that I was all in the past, and that the world was moving on without me.

Eggy went and sat down at her desk—well, it wasn't really a desk, it was more what they call a bedroom vanity unit, but Eggy used it as a desk. She wasn't that vain, really. Pretty (not that I ever said that to her) but not vain. That is, she didn't spend her whole life looking at herself in the mirror, not like some people.

She had some photographs of me up on the wall. Some of them were years old, and she must have dug them out since I'd been dead, because I was sure they hadn't been up there before.

She was working on some history essay. Her books were open on the vanity unit, and she had a writing pad there and some pencils at the ready for making notes.

As I watched, she sat back down on her chair and took up her history book. But much as she tried to read it, and much as she tried to concentrate, her eyes kept glancing up at those old photographs. There were photographs of me on my own and photographs of the two of us together. There was also a photo of when Eggy was small and when I was only a baby—maybe I'd even just been born. And she was holding me, with Dad's help, while Mum looked on, rather nervously, as if worried that Eggy might drop me on my head. (And maybe she even wanted to drop me on my head, just a bit.) Then there were later photos of her and me, both of us getting bigger and older. And she was always three years ahead of me, always my big sister, and I was always her pesky little brother, driving her nuts and getting on her nerves.

There were photographs of holidays, photographs of family occasions, photographs of Christmas and of birthdays, both hers and mine. There were photographs of cakes and conjurers and real little kiddy stuff that we had long since put behind us. There were photographs of all of us, too, of me and Eggy and Mum and Dad, all standing there together, smiling at the new camera with the automatic timer.

There I was. And there we were. And nothing would ever bring us back or make us whole again.

I felt so sad again—but I wouldn't give in to it. I was on a mission, like they say, and I had to see it through. I had to settle the unfinished business. I had to forgive and be forgiven. I couldn't let Eggy go through the rest of her life remembering those last words she'd ever said to me, just before I stormed out to get run over by a truck.

"You'll be sorry one day when I'm dead," I'd said to her.

"No, I won't be!" she'd shouted after me. "I'll be glad!"

And then I'd never come back.

"Eggy," I said. "Eggy, it's Harry. I'm here, right by you. Right here. But don't be afraid. It's OK, Eggy, I'm a ghost now, that's all. But it's OK, it's nothing to be frightened of. I'm not going to haunt you forever. I just came back to make it up with you, to say I'm sorry. Can you hear me, Eggy? Do you know I'm here?"

But she looked back down at her history book and reached out and turned a page over, and she didn't know that I was standing right behind her, so close that I could reach out and touch her.

"I'm touching your shoulder, Eggy. Can you feel my hand? Can you? It's me, Harry. Don't be afraid. I'm just touching your shoulder, that's all."

But she went on reading the history book, and then paused, and took up one of the pencils, and made a few notes about Henry the Eighth and all the wives he once had and why he had them.

"Eggy—it's me."

It was no use. There was no way I could make contact. When I thought of Alt and how just the sight of me had made all his fur stand on end, I did wonder why cats could be so sensitive and humans so thick-skinned. But if that's how it was, there didn't seem a lot I could do about it. A cat's a cat and a person's a person, and it's not as if you can turn one into the other at the touch of a button or the wave of a wand.

"Eggy . . ."

Nothing.

She looked up from her book, daydreaming, maybe, like you do in the middle of your homework. Her eyes fell on the photo of her and me at my fourth birthday party. Me getting ready to blow out all the candles, her getting ready to help me in case I ran out of puff.

"Oh, Harry," she said. "Oh, Harry."

And she reached out and touched the photo, just like it was flesh and blood and not just paper and chemicals.

I saw the pencil lying on the desk. I remembered the leaf on the tree, Jelly's pen, and Arthur with the fruit machine. I could do it. I knew I could. I had to.

I focused my thoughts on the pencil, all of them,

165

every part of me. I tried to shine my thoughts upon it as if they were the beam of a flashlight.

"Please," I thought, "please, please, *please* . . ."

And then I did it. It moved. The pencil *moved*. I moved it up onto its point, and it balanced there in the air, just as if some ghostly hand was around it, which—in a sense—it was.

"My *god!*" Eggy gasped, and she pushed her chair back. I wanted to think at her, "Don't worry, Eggy, don't be afraid," but I had no thoughts to spare. Everything of me was concentrating on that pencil, on holding it upright in the air, and then on making it move toward the paper of the pad.

Eggy remained in her chair. Frightened and yet—yet not frightened. Just waiting. Waiting to see. She had her hands on the edge of the desk, and was leaning back in her chair, almost as if she was trying to push the desk away.

But she didn't scream, she didn't run, she didn't shout for Mum and Dad, she just sat there, stiffly watching as the pencil began to move toward the paper. As it did, she said, "Harry? Harry? Is it you?"

I moved the pencil to the paper, and I made it write the word *Yes*.

She didn't turn, she kept her eyes on the pencil and the writing pad.

"Harry," she said. "I'm so sorry, Harry, I'm so sorry for what I said to you. I've thought about it ever since. Every second of every day. I'd do anything to undo it, Harry. I wish I could turn the clock back. I'm so sorry, Harry, I am."

And I made the pencil write, *I know. I'm sorry, too, Eggy.*

The writing was like my writing had been when I was alive, only it was very faint and spidery. I didn't have the mental strength somehow to put much pressure on the pencil. Just making the pencil write and keeping it in the air was taking all the strength I had, and I didn't know if I could hold it there for much longer. I already felt exhausted, as if there wasn't much of me left.

I thought at the pencil as hard as I ever could. And you know, making that pencil move across the paper was the most difficult thing I'd done in my entire—well, life.

Forgive me, Eggy, I wrote. *Please. For what I said.*

For a moment, she didn't say anything, she just sat, staring at the words on the paper, but then she swallowed hard and she said, "Of course I forgive you, Harry. Of course I do. Forgive me, too, won't you, Harry? You know I didn't mean it, don't you? I was angry. I said a stupid thing. Forgive me, Harry. I love you."

My strength was all but gone. I tried to force the pencil over the paper, to make it write down what I wanted to say. I tried, I really did try, you can't say I didn't try, no one could say that. And I almost did it, too, I almost did.

I love you, too, Eg—

And then the pencil fell before I could finish her name, and I couldn't write anymore.

"Harry? Are you still there?"

She turned and looked around the room.

"Harry?"

And of course I was till there, but all my strength had gone. And there was no more left to be said or done.

There was no more that I could say to the living. And little use in them saying anything to me.

And I felt it was time for me to go now.

To go and never to come back.

But I felt at peace at last. Sad and sorry, but at peace. I'd made it up with Eggy, and that made me feel as if a great weight had gone from me. And I remembered something that our headmaster, Mr. Hallent, had said once, during one of his boring assemblies, when he'd read this bit from the Bible about "Never let the sun go down on your wrath," meaning that you should never go to sleep still angry and enemies with someone, especially someone you loved. Because one of you might not wake up in the morning. And then where would you be? Well, I'll tell you. You'd be stuck with a whole big plateful of unfinished business, just like me.

Only my business was finished now. I'd said I was sorry. I could go now, move on to whatever lay there beyond the Other Lands, to whatever lay at the margins, past the eternal sunset. I could go off into the Great Blue Yonder.

"Bye, Eggy," I said. "Bye now. Have a good life. Don't worry about me. I'm OK. It happens to us all sometime. It happens to us all eventually. It just happened to me a bit sooner than I expected. But don't worry. Don't be sad for me. I'm OK. I've made some friends. I'm not alone. Bye, Eggy, bye."

"Harry," she said, standing looking around the room, "are you still there? I love you, Harry. I always did. Even when we fought each other. I'm sorry about the notice on the door. You were welcome in my room anytime. And to borrow my pens and my pencils and all my crayons and anything. Really, honest, you were—Harry?"

And then I kissed her on the cheek, and gave her one of my ghostly hugs, and I hurried out through the door. I didn't look back, I didn't hang around. I can't stand those long goodbyes. I think it's best to get it over with quickly myself. I know it might seem a bit abrupt and callous, even. But I think it's all for the best.

I went down to the kitchen and I said goodbye to Mum and Dad, and I hugged and kissed them both and I told them that I loved them and missed them and how I wished that they could see me one last time.

But I didn't stay long there, either.

You see, I wanted to remember them as they were. As they had been, when we had all been together. Happy, and not sad and sorrowful like they were now, probably just as they wanted to remember me.

I left the house and went on down the road without a backward glance. I'm not such a tough person, really, but I can be tough when I have to be, when it's what's needed. Sometimes you have to be tough like that, you see. Even hurt yourself a little bit, so as not to hurt even more later on.

As I passed through the playing fields, I spotted Alt the cat again, perched halfway up a tree, as if he'd decided to be a bird for a while.

"See you, Alt," I called to him. "Maybe see you around."

But his fur stood all on end again, and his paws went shooting off in all directions, and he looked like one of those flying squirrels that you see on nature programs as he launched himself into space, fell to the ground—probably losing a good four and a half of his nine lives in the process—and then was off across the football field at a million miles an hour.

And that was the last I saw of him.

And then it started to rain. I took shelter under a tree. Not because I was going to get wet or anything, but just for the pleasure of watching the rain come down, and of doing an ordinary thing, just like I was still alive.

It was quite a downpour, but you could tell that it wasn't going to last for long. The sky was already clearing in the distance, and the gray was giving way to blue. And after about ten minutes the rain stopped and the sun came out.

And then there, at the far end of the football field, was what I had been hoping for—a huge, glorious, magnificent rainbow.

I hurried toward it, as fast as I could go, intending to make my way back to the Other Lands, as soon as I possibly could.

The Great Blue Yonder

It was a bit like going on an escalator. Or maybe more like riding a roller coaster. Only instead of gathering speed on the downhill stretch, you gathered speed on the *uphill* one. And that was how I felt as I soared up along the rainbow, going so fast I went dizzy. And just as I got to the peak of the curve, I parted company with it and sailed on through a long dark tunnel of blackness and stars. And the next thing I knew, I was back in the Other Lands, standing at the far end of a very long queue for the Desk.

"Excuse me," I said. "Can I get by?"

Most of the people waiting in the queue were twice my size, and most of them were over fifty years old, at least. A lot of them looked cross, or baffled, with a *Why me?* look on their faces, and they all seemed impatient with the time the queue was taking to move. They maybe felt that they had waited in enough queues and traffic jams to last them a lifetime, and didn't want even more of them now that they were dead.

"Oi!"

"Where're *you* going?"

"Hey, watch him! He's pushing in."

I ducked and darted along, squirming by them, crawling under their legs sometimes. I thought I'd be able to walk through them, but I couldn't. It was odd, that, the way you could walk straight through something that was solid, but you couldn't walk through another ghost.

"Oi! Get to the back of the queue, you!" a large lady said. And she made a grab for me, but she was too slow, and I hurried on my way.

Not everyone tried to stop me. Some just tut-tutted to register their indignation.

"No manners," they said. "No manners at all. Kids today, pushing in everywhere and not waiting their turn."

Someone even called after me, "Hey! What are you doing being dead, anyway? You've not business being dead, a young lad like you!"

But I felt that I had no time for explanations, and I couldn't be bothered to give them, anyway, I'd done all the explaining I wanted to. I wasn't going to do any more.

"Excuse me!" I said, "excuse me," as I wriggled toward the front. "I'm not pushing in, I've been dead quite a while. Honest. I've already registered. I have."

"*Registered?* What do you mean, *registered?*" one of the newcomers said. "What's he on about?"

I pushed on. A man called after me.

"Hey, you there—boy!" he said. "What's at the end of the queue? Is there anyone in charge here? Because if there is, I want a word with them. There's been some mistake, you know. I shouldn't be dead at all."

But I hurried on.

"I shouldn't be dead, either," I heard someone say. "I left a pan on the stove. I ought to get back to switch it off, or it'll boil over."

"What about me?" another voice wailed. "I was due to go on my holidays. I'd saved up all year for that, and now I won't get to go."

Then I heard another voice, thin and reedy and very frail. It was the voice of an old, old man.

"I wouldn't go back for any price," he said. "I lived a long time and I had a good run. But come the end, I'd had enough of it and all my friends had died. So I enjoyed it, but I'm glad it's over now. It was getting to be a burden there, come the end. So I can't say I'm sorry."

I left them all to their arguing.

"Excuse me!" I said. "Can I get past? May I squeeze by, please. Sorry to bother you." The end was in sight. I could see the Desk now. There were just a few more people to go. "Excuse me! I'm not pushing in. I've already given my name."

"Then how come you're still in the line?" a lady asked.

But I just went on. I didn't feel up to answering their questions. I still had a few to ask myself. Like what happened when you reached the far horizon, where the sun was always setting, and what—if anything—lay beyond the Great Blue Yonder.

I was almost level with the Desk now. The same man was still there with his books and ledgers and his computer.

"Next!" he said mournfully to the next person in the queue as he shuffled forward.

"Here."

"Name!"

And so it went on.

I ducked down so as he wouldn't see me, and scurried past the desk. He looked up from his computer terminal and spotted me, though, and he let out a great cry.

"Oi! *You!*" he shouted. "I know you! Where have you been? Have you been back down there paying visits? That's against the rules, I'll have you know. Oi, you there! Oi! Come back!"

He stood up as if he might leave his desk and come after me, but plainly he couldn't, not with all those people standing waiting to give him their names, and more on the way every second. So I hurried along and I ignored all this bellowing for me to come back so that he could give me a good ticking-off.

And there I was, back in the Other Lands. Back in the dim, half-lit Other Lands. And there was nothing for it now but to head for the distant sunset and to find the Great Blue Yonder and to do whatever needed to be done.

So on I went. I didn't feel too bad. I wasn't sad, I wasn't happy, I wasn't anything, really, just neutral. I certainly didn't feel alive, and yet I didn't feel particularly dead, either. I didn't feel lonely, and yet I didn't feel not lonely. I could think of Eggy and Mum and Dad and I didn't feel upset anymore. I mean, I *was* upset, but not like I had been before I'd gone back and said goodbye to everyone and tried to make things right.

I think that's important somehow, being able to say goodbye and being able to make things right. It doesn't seem so bad if you've said goodbye. You feel you can cope with it then, you feel you can manage.

I walked on. Not going too slowly, yet not in any hurry, either. I wouldn't have minded a bit of company, and though there were plenty of people going the same way as me, I didn't really know or recognize anyone. I could have started up a conversation, I suppose, but it seemed a bit late to be making new friendships, and I longed for a familiar face.

I went on for a while, and as I turned a corner I saw Ug, the caveman. He was still wandering around the Other Lands, just as when I'd last seen him, still searching for whatever or whoever he'd lost. Maybe it was his long-dead pet dinosaur, maybe it was a saber-toothed tiger he'd once known, maybe it was a woolly mammoth. Maybe he'd had a pet dodo, back before they became extinct. Maybe it was Mrs. Ug he was looking for, or Grandma Ug, or all the baby Ugs, who wouldn't, of course, be baby Ugs anymore. They'll all have been big strong cavemen and cavewomen themselves, and dead for ten thousand years.

It seemed a long time to be searching for someone, ten thousand years.

He came up to me, as if I could maybe help.

"Ug," he said, and he waved his arms around. And then he said it again. "Ug! Ug! Ug!"

But I couldn't understand a word of it. There was no use in saying "Ug" to me. "Ug" just meant "Ug" as far as I knew, though I was sure that it meant something else to him.

"I'm sorry," I said. "But I can't really help. I wish I could. Sorry." And maybe the way he heard it, what I'd said sounded like a load of "Ug"s, too, a load of "Ug"s *he* didn't understand. And I really wished that I could speak fluent Ug and that they'd maybe taught it at our school. But they hadn't, and I didn't, and there was nothing I could do to help.

"Sorry, Mr. Ug," I said. "I only wish I could help. But I hope that you find what you're looking for. I really do."

And he gave me a sad, wistful look, and he shook his head, and he went on his way, still looking for whatever he'd lost, still trying to settle his unfinished business. So he went on his way, and I went on mine.

The sunset was getting nearer. I didn't have so far to go. I mean, in a way, time doesn't matter once you're dead; in some ways, there's no time at all. But just the same, things do seem to *take* time, even when there isn't really any time to take.

I turned another corner and I started to think about Arthur and whether he'd found his mum yet, and whether I'd ever see him again, or whether he'd popped back down to Earth, or maybe he'd fallen off his rainbow, or maybe he'd decided enough was enough and had gone off to the Great Blue Yonder.

Or maybe he'd decided to move in with Stan and spend the rest of eternity sitting in a flower basket, dangling from that lamppost, keeping an eye out for Winston the dog.

Then I saw him. He wasn't that far ahead of me. He was sort of slouched over and moping along. His top hat wasn't as jaunty-looking as usual, and his hands were stuffed in his pockets, and though I couldn't see his face, even the back of him looked pretty glum.

"Ar—"

I was just about to call his name when something

stopped me dead in my tracks. And it had stopped Arthur, too. Walking toward him was a woman. Quite a young, pretty woman, dressed in an old-fashioned costume, wearing one of those old dresses with a bit of a bustle at the back, like you see in those things on the telly.

She was walking slowly, and she looked sort of sad— sad the way Ug had looked, sad the way Stan had looked, sad the way Arthur's back looked—like she had some unfinished business that could never be resolved.

But then she saw Arthur, and she stopped. She stopped right there. And Arthur stopped, and I stopped, too. Neither of them was aware of me, and I was afraid to move. I just stood there, just like a statue of myself.

Arthur was fumbling in his coat, searching frantically through his pockets, getting all agitated, like he might have lost what he was looking for.

But I knew what he was looking for. He was looking for that button. The ghost of the button. The one he'd been given when he was only a baby. The one that was supposed to have come off his mum's blouse. His mum, who had died when he was born. The mum he had never known.

Arthur fumbled desperately for the button. As he did, I looked at the pretty, young woman in the old-fashioned clothes, and you could see that on her blouse was a line of pearl buttons—not real pearl, but pearly ones, the sort that Pearly Kings and Queens used to sew on to their clothes in the old days.

And I saw that there was a button missing, there at the top, and at her neck her collar was held together with a pin.

Arthur stopped fumbling. He'd found it. He'd found the button, buried somewhere in the deep recesses of his pocket. He held the button out flat on his hand, and he looked from it to the buttons on the lady's blouse. And it must have been the same, it must have been *just* the same. Because he took a step forward, still holding the button out, holding it for the lady to see.

"Mum?" he said. "Mum, is it you?"

And the lady stepped toward him, too, and she picked up the button from his outstretched hand, and she held it next to one of the pearly buttons on her blouse. And you could see they were the same, just the same, the very same buttons. And I knew then that they had found each other, after all those years of roaming the Other Lands. After all those years of wrong turnings and near misses, they had found each other at last.

"Mum?" Arthur said. "It is you, isn't it? It's really you."

"Yes," she said, "it's me, Arthur, it's me."

I turned away. It only seemed right. I didn't think it was my business. It seemed only proper to give them some time alone together, after all the years they'd been apart. They had a lot to catch up on, after all—all the news and the rest.

But after a while I started to make clearing-my-throat noises, until eventually they had to notice me. And when Arthur saw who it was, he called me over and introduced me to his mum. And he seemed dead proud of her and pleased with her, even if she did have a button missing. And I felt a bit envious in a way, that he had his mum with him and I didn't have mine. Just for a moment I wished that I'd been able to introduce my mum, too.

Then I realized that in order for that to happen, she'd have to be dead as well. And I didn't want that to happen, so I stopped thinking about it.

I asked Arthur and his mum if they were thinking of going on anywhere else, now that they'd met each other at last. They said that they thought they might as well go on to the Great Blue Yonder now, as there was no further need to go wandering the Other Lands like lost souls. So I said that I was thinking of going that way myself, and would they mind if I walked along with them? And they said no, it would be a pleasure to have the company. Which was what I'd been hoping they'd say all along.

So on we went, on toward the everlasting sunset, the eternal twilight which never got brighter or darker but which just always was.

There was quite a crowd of people going along in the same direction now. All sorts and sizes and all ages, too. And none of them seemed sad, and while none of them looked happy exactly, they all seemed to be at peace. It was like they had all reached a decision, and their minds were at rest.

I started to ask a few people what exactly we might be going to, and just what lay beyond the Great Blue Yonder. Not many seemed to know, exactly, but Arthur's mum said that it was like becoming part of life again, and I asked her what she meant.

"It's sort of like a leaf, Harry," she said. "a leaf in a forest. You know, the way it falls from a tree. Because what happens to it, then?"

"It dies, I suppose," I said.

"Yes, that's true," she said. "It does. But it doesn't,

really. Because it becomes part of the soil again, part of life, and new trees grow, with new leaves. And we're like that, too."

I started to get all excited then.

"You mean I'll get to go *back?*" I said. "You mean I'll get to have another go? That I'll come back as another leaf—I mean, as another Harry?"

She gave me a bit of a smile and shook her head.

"No, not really, Harry. Not quite like that. You will come back, but not as you are. It's more that, well—it's the way the leaves return to the ground—you'll be in everything and everyone. Just the way that everyone and everything was once part of you."

"Was it?" I said, a bit mystified.

"Yes," she said. "I think so."

And then there we were. I don't know how to describe it, really. We just sort of came to the end of the Other Lands, and there we all were, watching this glorious sunset, and the sun was setting over the bluest, clearest, greatest sea I had ever seen.

We stood there on a headland and there the sea was below us. And yet it wasn't really a sea, not as you know them when you're alive. It wasn't water, just a sort of force, just, well, like a great ocean of—life, I suppose.

I stood there a while and thought about what Arthur's mum had said. So I'd come back. I wouldn't be a ghost forever. I'd come back. I'd live on, in people's thoughts and memories, and everything I'd ever done and everything I'd ever been would have made a difference. Not necessarily a big difference, but a difference just the same.

And when I waded in now, and became part of that great blue ocean, I wouldn't be me anymore, but I'd be part of the stuff that made new life, and I'd all go into making new thoughts, and new people.

And I thought that maybe that wasn't so bad.

I thought of Mum and Dad then. I remembered Dad in the kitchen saying to Mum how he wished they'd maybe had another baby. And I thought that when some time had gone by, maybe they would.

And maybe—if I became part of the great blue ocean now—some of me would go into that baby, too. I mean, I didn't expect *all* of me to go into it. Obviously the baby would be a person in its own right. But maybe there'd be a *little* bit of me there, just a little, just a dash of Harry.

And you know what I imagined, then? Well, I imagined that baby as he (or maybe it would be she) grew up, along with Mum and Dad and my sister, Eggy. And I imagine how, as the baby got older, as he started to crawl and to walk and talk, that every now and again he would do something, and my mum would turn to my dad and say, "You know—you know who he puts me in mind of when he does that?"

And my dad would nod, and he'd know straightaway, and he'd say, "Yes, you're right. I've thought that myself, too. He puts you in mind of Harry."

And when he was older, and better able to understand, they'd tell him about this brother he had but who he never knew. And they'd say, "You'd have liked him, and he'd have liked you. You've got the same sense of humor, you two. Yes, you'd have liked your brother Harry. You would."

And he would.

And I'd have liked him, too.

Arthur and his mum seem to have gone.

I can hear the sound of seagulls, but I can't see any. Maybe I'm just imagining it.

I think I heard Arthur and his mum say goodbye a moment ago. I think I even called back and waved. I was a bit lost in my thoughts. And then they were off into the Great Blue Yonder, just like birds taking off into the sky.

So here I am. I'm right here on the headland, looking out toward that deep, beautiful blue.

I'm standing here and I'm thinking as hard as I can. As hard as I did when I moved the pencil in Eggy's room and told her I was sorry. I'm thinking my thoughts as hard as I can think them. I'm trying to broadcast them out, the way a radio transmitter sends out its signal, and I'm hoping that someone will be on my wavelength, and that I can put my thoughts into their mind.

I would like someone to tell my story. No one ever does, do they? Not for most ordinary people. People live and people die, and no one tells their story. They think that just because you're ordinary, you can't be interesting. But I don't think that's so. So I'm hoping that someone will hear me, that's all.

So I'll say goodbye now. Goodbye to you all. And if you're going to ride a bike on a busy road, you will be careful, won't you? Double careful if you can. And remember to check the laces on your shoes *before* you set off, OK? Though accidents can happen no matter what you do, and that's the truth.

Anyway, I'll say goodbye now. Goodbye to Mum and to Dad and to Eggy, to Alt the cat, and to all my friends. I didn't have a bad life. I know it was short. But don't feel sorry for me. I'm OK. I'm just sorry for the people I left behind, that's all, because they're so sad that I've gone.

But listen, one last thing. You know, you mustn't be afraid—of being dead, I mean. Because look at me. I mean, to be honest, I know I act all tough sometimes, and I bet you think I'm a real hard case, but deep down inside you won't get a bigger scaredy-cat or a bigger crybaby than me. But I've been all right. I've managed. So, honestly, it's nothing to worry about, not once it's happened. And once it *has* happened, what can you do about it, anyway? So don't be afraid. It's OK. Honestly. We're all right. Don't worry. Don't be sad for us. We're OK. And don't be afraid when it's time to join us, because that's all right, too.

Bye, then. Thanks for listening. That's almost the end of my story now. And any second, it'll be the end of me. I'm going off now, off into the Great Blue Yonder, just like a leaf becoming part of the soil, just like Arthur's mum said. I'm off to become part of everything that gives us life. And I won't be Harry anymore. But that doesn't mean you won't see me. I'll still be there. I'll be there in the school and the park and I'll be there on the football field and I'll be there in all the photographs and memories.

Anyway, I'm just rambling now, just going on for the sake of it, just to put it off a moment longer. Just like I did that day I dived off the top board. Anything but go.

OK.

OK.

That's it. I really mean it this time. My mind's made up. I'm away now. Away into the Great Blue Yonder.

Bye, Mum, bye, Dad, bye, Eggy. I miss you. I love you all. I love you all so much. I love you all so very, very much, more than words can ever say.

Here I go, then. Here I go. The great blue ocean lies beneath me.

So here I go.

Here I go now. I'm really going to do it this time.

Watch me. Watch this now. I'm going any minute.

And remember, don't worry. It's OK. We'll be all right.

So I'm going now.

I'm going this time.

I'm going.

I really am.

I am.

I mean it.

Here goes, then.

Wish me luck.